SISTER WIFE

A totally addictive psychological thriller
with a shocking twist

ANYA MORA

The Sister Wife Domestic Suspense Thrillers Book 1

Originally published as
The Sister Wife's Secret

JOFFE BOOKS

Revised edition 2024
Joffe Books, London
www.joffebooks.com

First published as *The Sister Wife's Secret* in the USA in 2021

This paperback edition was first published
in Great Britain in 2024

This book is a work of fiction. Names, characters, businesses, organizations, places and events are either the product of the author's imagination or are used fictitiously. Any resemblance to actual persons, living or dead, events or locales is entirely coincidental. The spelling used is American English except where fidelity to the author's rendering of accent or dialect supersedes this.

Cover art by Nebojša Zorić

ISBN: 978-1-83526-438-6

CHAPTER 1

There's no such thing as perfect. I know that. But it doesn't stop me from fluffing the pillows on the secondhand sofa, meticulously arranging the tray of fresh veggies and dip, and lining up each clipboard on the coffee table in a straight line. Setting a blue ball-point pen on each one.

The papers clipped to the boards explain everything the ladies who are coming to my home party tonight need to know about joining this *fun and exciting new venture.*

I need to work on that wording. It sounds a little too salesman-y. And that isn't what I'm after. I'm trying to share this amazing business opportunity with my friends so they can reap all the same benefits as me.

Okay. That's equally pitchy.

"Mom!" Ruthie shrieks, running into the kitchen where I'm adding ground beans to a pot for decaf coffee. "Olive's trying to scare me!"

At eight, Ruthie has perfected melodrama. I don't mind. I like seeing my youngest daughter express herself. After so many years of burying our emotions, I'm here for this.

Olive, twelve, enters the room, rolling her eyes. "I wasn't trying to scare you. I was just being honest."

I twist my lips, flipping the coffee pot on. "Honest about what?"

"Olive told me to go to the basement, and then when I was down there, she turned off the lights and said there are ghosts. Is that true?"

I lift my eyebrows. "Olive, stop it, you're working her up for no reason. And I need you both on your best behavior tonight. The party is going to start in five minutes."

"No one's even here yet," Olive says, dipping a carrot in the ranch dressing.

I walk to the living room, peering out the window. No cars are pulling up. But I see a black sedan parked down the street. My throat goes dry at the sight. It has been pulling up there every night for a week.

Not wanting the girls to see my worry, I turn to them and shrug. "I think it's different here than it was at Garden Temple. Here, women have lots going on with their jobs, families, errands." It seems like everyone I talk to mentions being overwhelmed. It's a new concept for me. I grew up in a place where there was always time. Long, never-ending stretches of it.

"Which is why having sister wives is smart," Olive says, twisting her long blonde hair in her fingers. Her words sting. I didn't fight so hard to escape only to have Olive consider our old life preferable to the one we have now. But I don't let my irritation show. My daughter needs time to get over the indoctrination she grew up with. Olive sidles up next to me, looking through the window, out at the neighborhood. It's a far cry from the compound. Here there are green grass lawns, SUVs in every driveway, street lamps glowing down on the street — making sure everyone and everything is seen. There are no secrets here. Everything is out in the open.

It's why I moved to this home two months ago, leaving the rundown apartment we'd been at for the year after running away. I was determined to move my girls from the shady apartment complex, even if it meant we were house poor. Rent is more than half my paycheck.

Which is why I've started this home business. wELLEness is a line of wellness products, created by a woman named Elle Christopher. Organic, essential, and life-giving products, at least that was what Anna, the woman who signed me up for this business, claimed. After I tried a cough syrup when Olive came down with a bad cold, I was hooked. The products sell themselves, truly.

"Sister wives may be good for lots of things," I say, pushing away my feelings. I miss Lydia and Beth so much it hurts. "But not everything."

Olive purses her lips, acting like the preteen she is, and shrugs. "It's better than this. It's boring here."

I exhale, frustrated with her. Children are a blessing, but my God, are they stubborn. And Olive is just like her father. She digs in her heels and can't see any other point of view.

Ruthie smiles, mischief in her eyes. "It's not boring. We live in a haunted house, right?"

Olive laughs. "I really didn't mean to scare you."

The phone rings and I head to the kitchen to grab it. I got a landline for the girls when I'm at work, but no one has the number. Sure it's a telemarketer, I tell them to take me off their list, but after I say my piece, there's no response. Just heavy breathing and then a click. The call ends.

"Who was it?" Olive asks, close on my heels.

"No one," I say, but my gut knows that's not true. Jeremiah may have finally found me. I consider pulling out my phone and calling Patrick, texting him at least to see where he is. He's supposed to be here tonight, helping me with the party.

We aren't dating, he's never even made a move . . . but I know he cares for me and my girls. He's done plenty over the last few months to show me his character — he's wealthy, sure, but he is also generous. And I know if I felt unsafe, he would do anything to help me feel protected.

Over the last two months as we've grown closer, I've tried to open up with him about my past . . . but it's hard. Now, though, maybe I need to get over that. Sure, opening up means letting myself be vulnerable, but it also means having someone in my corner. And right now I could use a champion.

As if reading my mind, my phone buzzes in my pocket. I pull it out and there's a text from Patrick.

Patrick Kelly: *I'm so sorry Gray. I can't make it. But I've been thinking about you all day and know you'll do great!*

All day? Seems intense. I want a friendship with Patrick, but not more. I'm not exactly sure how to say that. I'm new to all this. Friendships with women, I understand. But men? I've never had a man in my life besides Jeremiah.

But that isn't what really bothers me.

He isn't coming. My stomach flip-flops. I was not prepared to do this alone.

Me: *What do you mean? Is everything okay?*

Patrick Kelly: *Things are fine — but I got held up with work. Treydon and Anna messed up an order — they're here now helping to fix it. I'll tell you about it in person.*

My thumbs hover over the keyboard, unsure of how to reply.

Patrick Kelly: *Let's go on a walk tomorrow morning on Ruston Way. 9?*

I consider the next morning. The groceries can wait. And I know Patrick will want to talk about the party, the wellness products are his whole life. He's the top wELLEness recruiter in all of Washington state. It's why his sister Anna started selling in the first place.

Me: *Sounds good. Meet at your place?*

He sends me a thumbs up.

I put my phone away as a neighbor walks up the driveway. I exhale, desperate for the night to go as smoothly as possible. This is my first home party and Patrick isn't here to help. I'm flying solo.

The girls notice the way I draw in a sharp breath. They know all my tells. That I'm worried.

Leaving Garden Temple was the most difficult thing I've ever done, and I've spent many nights scared that Jeremiah would find us, force us back. But I never want to see that man again. He made me his wife when I was just fourteen years old. When I heard rumors of plans for Olive's betrothal, I knew I needed to leave.

Even if it meant tearing my children away from the only life they've ever known.

Well, two of my children.

Abel is still there. Living in his father's shadow.

But I can't think on that now. Not when more cars are pulling up and women are walking to the front door.

Ruthie gives me a hug. "You'll be great, Mom."

Olive, though, isn't as excited for my new venture. She misses her old life, and a night where women are gathering only reminds her of what used to be our everyday normal. "I'm going to my room. Come on, Ruthie." She reaches for her little sister's hand. My heartstrings tug. She may be unhappy about my choices, but she isn't taking them out on her sister.

I put on a smile as I open the front door of my 1920s Gladstone home. It's rough around the edges, compared to my neighbors' updated houses, but I've done my best to make it cozy. The landlord had no issue with me painting the bedrooms, which meant the world to the girls.

"Hi, Gray," Julia says, already on the front porch. I let her into the house. She lives four doors down and her daughter Cleo is in Ruthie's class. Most mornings before school I see her outside, pushing a jogging stroller with her toddler. "Thanks for the invite." Julia's wearing leggings and a down vest, sporty shoes, and her blonde hair in a ponytail. She looks like she lives in an athletic clothing catalogue.

"Of course, I'm glad you could make it."

"Oh, this was on the doorstep." She hands me a white envelope, sealed, but unaddressed.

I frown turning it over. Then I tuck it in the pocket of my dress as Kendall greets us both.

"Hey, ladies," she says. "I brought wine. Is that okay?" She hands me a bottle of white and I take it, nodding more than necessary.

"Of course, come on in," I say. A few other moms from the block join us, Luna and Avery. In the kitchen I offer everyone coffee. "Or wine," I say, biting my bottom lip, eyeing the bottle. Grateful the cap can twist off. I don't own a corkscrew. Old habits die hard.

"Oh God, wine please," Kendall says. She laughs, loud. "It's been a day. Savannah threw a huge fit at Costco, then Gordie legit refused a bottle. And when I got Audrey from school, she started crying because of some playground drama. I was like, girl, I'm the one who could use a good cry, not you!"

The other moms laugh and I pull out my mason jars that I use as water glasses. They will have to do for the wine.

"Thanks, Gray," Julia says, taking a jar from my hand. "Your place is like a literal Pinterest board."

The women all nod in agreement, taking in my felt letter board with the words FOLLOW YOUR HEART pressed in. I made the seasonal wreath over the fireplace, cutting out the red and white hearts for Valentine's Day that's in two weeks. I found lace doilies at the thrift shop and crocheted them together, making shabby chic curtains for the kitchen.

"I've always liked to craft," I say, not wanting the attention.

"How do you do it all?" Avery asks as we take our plates of snacks and drinks to the living room. "I swear, by the end of the day I'm exhausted. I used to scrapbook before we had the twins, but now?" She laughs. "I'm lucky to shower."

We find seats and my stomach flip-flops, eyeing the clipboards. I need to sell them on these supplements and getting too off track might make them forget the reason for this get-together.

"Doing crafts is my version of self-care, I suppose," I say, using the phrase that I hear these women reference constantly. "It's cheaper than therapy."

They laugh, understanding, and just like that, we've found common ground.

"So, show us these supplements or whatever," Julia says. "Oh, and my sister-in-law in California is obsessed with Moon-Mask. Do you have that?"

I smile, grateful for the segue. "Actually, I do. Moon-Mask is a face mask meant to clear your skin when you're on your cycle. Its formula includes St. John's wort and it's actually incredible. If you all want to take a peek at the clipboards in front of you . . ."

The next hour goes quickly. Relief washes over me as all the women place orders, and Kendall wins the door prize of 25% off her first purchase. I smile as I assess their purchases, stereotyping them each as I do.

Avery, who only a few months ago gave birth to twins, orders Sleep-Tight, a melatonin and horsetail-infused tea meant to help you go to sleep while tightening your skin.

Julia, the fitness lover, chooses a box of Sweet-Cheeks, the popular turmeric and pineapple juice meant to promote a healthy inflammatory response post-workout, and also lift the muscles in your buttocks.

Kendall, the over-extended mommy, opts for Glow-Up, a mood enhancing supplement with milk thistle that helps support glowing skin.

And Luna, the yoga-loving mother with older children and more time on her hands, picks Devotion-Potion, a hibiscus oil meant to help with meditation.

It isn't until I'm running their cards through Square on my phone that Luna asks where my girls are.

"Oh, they're asleep," I say, handing her back her Visa.

Her eyes lift. "Just like that? They put themselves to bed?"

I lick my lips. "They're good girls."

Luna slips her card back in her wallet. "Well, my Sophie is fifteen now and I can handle getting her out of bed for school, but when she was younger, she was never a good sleeper."

"Every kid is different, right?" I say. Not adding that at Garden Temple it wasn't a choice. Every child obeyed the rules. And there were lots of them. Going to bed on time wasn't difficult when the alternative was a punishment from their father. Spare the rod, spoil the child was an often-repeated phrase.

"You know," Avery says. "If you ever want a night off, Sophie is a great babysitter. She watches my kids for date night once a week."

I smile politely. "Well, I'm not going on dates at the moment so . . ."

Julia clucks her tongue. "You sure? I saw a man over here twice last week."

Heat rises to my cheeks. "Oh, that's just Patrick."

"*Just* Patrick?" Kendall asks, taking the last sip of wine in her glass.

"He's a friend is all." I stand and collect the empty plates and walk them to the kitchen.

"Sophie is really good with kids. Even if you just want a few hours to yourself," Avery says. "I'm texting you her number right now."

"Is there no man then?" Julia presses. "No father . . ."

Her words peter off and I feel the other ladies give her a hard look.

"Sorry," she says, cringing. "Seriously. You're new to the neighborhood is all and I wanted to get to know you better, but that's not the way to do it."

"It's okay," I say as the women head to the door. "And Ruthie and Olive's father? He's completely out of the picture."

Glancing back at the black sedan parked at the curb, I hope I'm right about that. Because something tells me he'll never be totally gone.

CHAPTER 2

The morning after the home party, I wake early. The girls are still asleep. Moving quietly so as not to wake them, I make their lunches, and then mix up pancake batter before starting a load of laundry. In the basement — the not-haunted one — I sort dirty clothes, emptying pockets before putting clothes in the wash. I find the envelope in my dress pocket, having completely forgotten it last night after everyone left.

The envelope is nondescript, but as I pull out the paper inside, I find that the words inside are more than memorable. They send a jolt of fear through me that I haven't felt since those first weeks after we left Garden Temple.

You won't get away with this.

Only one line printed on a yellow slip of paper, but a single sentence is all it takes for my stomach to drop. Who wrote this and why? Get away with what? My mind goes to the black sedan. The phone calls.

Jeremiah knows where I am.

"Mom?" Ruthie calls from the top of the stairs.

"I'm down here, honey. Just give me a sec," I say, shoving the paper in the back pocket of my jeans. I add detergent, then shut the lid to the washing machine, wishing the words on the paper could be washed away too.

Climbing the stairs, I mentally prepare myself for the day ahead. Drop the girls off at the bus, go grocery shopping, then head to the library downtown for my shift. I shelve books thirty hours a week, while the girls are at school.

"Pancakes?" Olive asks with a smile.

I nod. "With strawberries. My way of saying thank you for being so good last night."

"Did you sell any vitamins?" Ruthie asks, placing her lunch bag in her backpack.

"I did. Anna is going to be proud of me."

"I'm proud of you too, Mom," Ruthie says, grinning. She's so good to me it makes my heart ache. Being a mom is the privilege of my life, but she makes it easy.

"What would Father think? You working outside the home?" Olive asks as I flip a pancake.

I fight the urge to give a flippant reply. She is just a child, and she is testing me. Still, I can't bite my tongue entirely. "Technically, I wasn't working outside the home, Olive, was I?"

That has her fighting a smile, not used to seeing me snippy. To be honest, I think she respects me more when I add a little bite to my bark.

"The library, though—" she starts in again.

I shake my head. "Not today, sweetie. I'm grateful for my job. It affords us this life. This life where we are free. So please, I know you're angry, but don't take it out on me."

Olive drops her gaze, and nods. When I dish them up, they eat quietly. I pick up my phone, checking the text from Patrick last night, confirming what time we are meeting up. Nine a.m.

I smile, thinking how excited he will be to hear about my sales. I wish he'd been able to make it to the party, but I know he is going to be impressed. I slip my phone in my purse, turning back to the girls. "Ready to catch the bus?"

* * *

As I leave my street in Hilltop, my neighborhood in central Tacoma, I feel grateful to have found the rental I did. The area is growing and nearly every house on the block has been renovated or is in the middle of construction. It's a developing area in a large city an hour from Seattle. When I left Garden Temple, I considered my options. I'd spent my life in rural Eastern Washington and knew it would be difficult to get lost in a small town. I needed something bigger — but knew the apartments in Seattle were out of my price range.

Tacoma was closer to my budget, and still big enough a place to fade into the background. The job at the public library even fits that bill. Between shelves, I pass the hours unnoticed. Except by Anna Treble. She managed to pull me out of my shell when we met four months ago. She'd been looking for books on home canning, and I was able to help her understand the basics.

It was with her help that I found my rental home. Doris Jenkins, my landlord, is her family friend and I know it was Anna's good word that had her renting to me even though I didn't have both first and last months' rent for a deposit.

Anna also signed me up for *wELLEness* after telling me how she paid for her family's Christmas vacation to Disneyland with her home business income. And when the girls and I joined her family on New Year's Day for a chili cook-off, I met her brother Patrick.

Pulling up to Patrick's waterfront condo now, I try not to overthink things. He's a generous guy who's been good to me. And while he's a bit too flashy for my liking, he never pressures me to take our friendship somewhere I'm not ready for it to go.

To be honest, I can't imagine it ever going anywhere beyond morning walks and coffee dates. I've friend-zoned him, but it isn't because he isn't charming — it's because he's almost too perfect. His teeth too white, his condo too well-appointed. Everything brand-new and top of the line. It's not me.

When I get to his place, I knock on the door, peeking in through the window next to his door. When he doesn't come right away, I send him a quick text letting him know

I've arrived. I take a deep breath in, then exhale, shaking off the weird letter, the sedan from last night, determining to be present today.

The sun is out, which is welcome after so many rainy days, and while it's cold, there's no snow on the ground in February, which is different than how Garden Temple would look right now, on the other side of the mountains that cut across the state.

When several minutes pass without him opening the door, I frown, check my phone again, and then I walk to his carport to see if his car is here. His Tesla is parked where it always is. Not wanting to intrude, but also registering that this is unlike him, I walk around the complex, toward his backyard patio that faces Commencement Bay.

His BBQ is covered, and his outdoor furniture is wet from the rain the night before. For a moment everything looks as I'd expect.

But then I see the sliding glass door is smashed in, shards of glass scattered across the patio stones like drops of water.

My heart pounds as I step toward the smashed door. "Patrick?" I call out. Then louder, starker, I shout. "Patrick, are you here?"

I step into his home, fear winding up my spine. I've been scared before. Plenty of times. Scared when Jeremiah made me his wife when I was just fourteen. Scared of giving birth; it never got less terrifying, three times in a row I was petrified of what it would mean to bring a baby into the world in which I lived. Scared when I took the girls and fled.

But that was a different kind of fear than what I'm experiencing now. This is bone chilling. This is life or death.

Because on the beige carpet of his living room floor, Patrick lies, in his REI boots and Patagonia parka, ready for our walk.

With blood pooling around his head.

I move to him, this man I care about, this man who wanted to take care of me. I gasp, "Patrick." Dropping to my knees, my voice is thin, broken. But not like the sharp panes of glass. My voice is soft, a whisper, wanting to breathe life into this man who is gone.

His blood seeps into the carpet, into my clothes, as I search his face, trying to understand what happened. *Why* it happened.

There's a bullet wound at his temple, his eyes are still, his body cold. I lean down, holding on to him as if for dear life, but there is no life to hold on to. Not now. No. Patrick is dead.

CHAPTER 3

I've been in the presence of exactly two dead people in my life. My mother and my father. I was ten years old when they died in a car crash. I'd been in the car, too. A survivor, but it didn't feel that way. It felt like they left me. After they died I never slept another night in our home, never went back to my elementary school, and never had a chance to say goodbye to my neighborhood friends.

Instead I moved in with my aunt and uncle who lived at Garden Temple. In an instant, everything changed, forever.

But before the sirens roared, before a coroner took them away, and before I started a new life on a two-hundred-acre slice of so-called paradise, I crawled between the two front seats of the minivan, reaching for my mother's hand, my father's arm.

I begged my parents to turn and look at me. I wanted to see their faces more than anything. To memorize their smiles, their noses, their eyes. Panic had taken hold of me as I realized they were dead, gone, and I was scared I might already start to forget them.

But now, as I kneel before Patrick's lifeless body, hot tears filling my eyes, I blink them away. I'm not the little girl longing for her parents. That girl has long been buried.

Now, I am a woman who has faced more than death. I've lived through hell.

I reach for my phone in my purse, calling 911.

I give them the details, the address of where we are. I speak calmly, directly. I know how to stay in control even when it feels like everything is spiraling out. It's how I managed to escape Garden Temple.

"Ma'am," the operator says, her voice as neutral as mine. "I need you to remain on the line. Are you alone?"

"Uh, I think so," I say, my voice thick.

"And your name?"

"Gray. Gray West."

"I need you to stay where you are, Gray," she says calmly.

I already hear the faint whir of a siren in the distance and I stand, looking down at the only man I have ever befriended. Patrick was good to me, to my girls, and now . . . now he's gone. I can't go there now — to any emotion. Not now.

My instincts tell me I'm alone, but as I look around the living room, I consider the fact that a killer was here.

The last eighteen years of my life taught me to trust no one . . . but as I consider someone breaking and entering this luxury condo, I can't imagine why someone would have it out for Patrick.

The operator is still on the line, telling me to stay put, as I pull my keys from my purse, pushing them between my fingers, my eyes falling on a smashed photograph on the mantel.

The photograph of Patrick, Treydon and me at the new recruit banquet last month. Treydon is head of PR for wELLEness and I remember how he'd wrapped his arms around me, pulling Patrick and I closer.

"It's for Insta," he told me. "I'll tag you."

I told him I didn't have social media, and he laughed, shaking his head at me. Thinking I was a country bumpkin. He wasn't wrong. But it isn't why I'm not on the internet.

Later, he gave Patrick and I both a copy of the photo. I never realized Patrick had framed his. Mine is on the fridge at home.

"The officers will be there any moment," the operator tells me.

The glass of the picture frame is shattered, the photo pulled out, beside it. But not damaged. I don't touch it, the operator reminding me I am not to tamper with the crime scene.

"Okay," I reply, breathless, my stomach in knots as I walk around the first floor, through the shining stainless-steel kitchen, pushing open the bathroom door where even the hand towel hangs neatly. The operator says not to move, but I can't help myself. I need to see this condo one last time for myself.

Patrick's office is tidy, a chair parked behind a large desk. On a shelving unit there's a display of this season's special vitamins and elixirs. There's a tripod, a standing halo light, his props for taking photographs for his wELLEness social media accounts. Nothing's amiss, except for the desk drawer that's pulled open, revealing it is empty. I frown. Either someone was here and took something, or someone came looking and couldn't find what they wanted.

I'm no detective, not a sleuth by a long shot — but I do know about secrets, about lies, about pretending. Reaching to open the drawer beneath it, I startle as a loud voice fills the apartment.

"Tacoma PD," a booming voice calls.

I pull back my hand, clench my fists. What was I about to do? Dig up a motive for murder? It's absurd. All of this is. I was supposed to be taking a morning walk before work. Not finding Patrick dead.

"Hello," I say, walking into the living room, ending the call with the operator. Then I press my lips together as I take in the two male officers who were called to the scene. "I'm Gray West."

The shorter of the two men narrows his eyes. "Why were you walking around the crime scene?"

I shake my head, looking for an answer. There isn't a good one. Finally I land on something. "I didn't want to be in the room with him alone."

The officer's black hair is cropped short, his nose sharp. "Officer Truce," he says, shaking my hand. Then he lifts his chin to the other man. "This is York." He points to a man who looks like he's barely out of high school.

Taking off his hat, Truce steps closer, he flashes me his badge. "You were the one who made the 911 call?"

"Yes, I came here this morning to meet my friend Patrick for a walk," I explain. "But found this, found him . . . he's in the living room, over here."

Truce is already kneeling before Patrick, letting me know the medics have been dispatched.

I walk toward where the sliding glass had been; the sun shines through the broken panes of glass of the sliding door. Taunting me. There should have been a pleasant walk, with warmth around our shoulders, telling Patrick about my first home party, about my sales, how it was a success because of his and Anna's help.

I swallow. *Anna*. A chill creeps into the exposed room, up my spine. She's going to be devastated.

I turn, facing the men, suddenly feeling vulnerable — the very thing I've been fighting against my entire life. But here I am, alone with two men. Another man dead a few feet away.

They wear badges but that doesn't mean I'm safe. I know plenty about men in power. The bad ones are easy enough to identify. But even the ones you think are good usually aren't.

"Boone? What are you doing here?" Truce scowls, and I turn to see a man in a rumpled suit stepping through the broken door. He has reddish-brown hair, curly around the ears. A beard, broad shoulders. He would seem intimidating if it weren't for the freckles across his nose.

"I heard the call, was in the neighborhood."

"Nice beard," York says with a wry smile. "Guess the rumors are true. Really are having a mid-life crisis."

I swallow, wanting to be anywhere but here. Being alone with men I don't know isn't something I am used to.

"Detective Boone," the man says, offering me a callused hand. He looks like he belongs in the woods, not this modern condominium. And definitely not in a suit.

"Gray here was the one who made the call," Truce says. "And she was walking around the condo. So she isn't great at following directions."

None of this is funny — but the comment does have me making a dry laugh. Me, not good at following directions? These people know nothing about me.

"Get the coroner here," Boone says, his eyes darting to Patrick. You don't have to get close to know he is gone. "And you," he says to me. "Outside. I need to get your statement."

The next hour passes in a blur; Patrick leaves the apartment in a body bag. The ambulance pulls out of the parking lot, transporting Patrick to the morgue. I hate being here, questioned by officers who like digging a bit too much for my liking. My mind on the photo of Patrick and I, on the mantel, smashed. It was the only thing in the house that was destroyed.

Standing outside the condo, I wrap my arms around myself, trying to be as helpful as possible as Boone finishes asking me questions. Truce and York are still inside.

"Anna is the person you want to talk to, not me," I say to Boone. "His sister."

Boone stands in front of the sun, the brightness gleaming around him, making it hard for me to meet his eyes. I hold up a hand to shield the light.

"Right, Anna," he says. "And you were friends with both of them? For how long?"

"Only since this fall. I met Anna while I was at work."

He's writing this all down. "And where is that?"

"At the library downtown."

His eyes flick up. "Oh yeah?"

I nod, swallowing hard. I don't really want this man asking me anything else. I have enough secrets and don't exactly want a cop looking into my personal life. "Speaking of work, I need to go. Is there anything else you need from me?"

His pine-green eyes narrow slightly, and he steps closer to me, out from the sun, but now his gaze is fixed on me. He pulls a card from his wallet. "Listen, if you think of anything else that might be helpful, will you give me a call? Otherwise I've got your information and know how to find you."

I take the card from him, unsure of why it feels so strange, the way he is looking at me with intent. Does he think I'm hiding something?

I turn to leave but stop before I get very far. "Boone," I say, the vowels in his last name comforting somehow. Soft and long. "What happens to him now?"

"He goes to the coroner. Then his family can decide what they want to do next." He runs a hand over his beard. "Why?"

"It's just so final, isn't it?" I don't know why I turned back to Boone, why I opened my mouth, but I did.

He thinks I'm asking about the technical aspects of where a body goes after a murder. But the questions I have are the ones that aren't so easily defined. I became an adult in a place where there was only black and white. Heaven or hell. Good or evil. Sinner or saint.

Now, though, I live in the gray, the in-between. And I realize I don't even know what Patrick believed. How close were we if I don't know something as simple as that?

"Do you need to talk to someone?" Boone asks. "There are counselors I can—"

I cut him off. "No thank you," I say, pushing my emotions back down. I hardly knew Patrick. But I don't need a therapist to analyze this. I'm emotional over so much more. All the things I've lost. The things that were taken. This feels like just one more to add to the pile.

I hear Jeremiah's cold voice. *"You always manage to make it about you, don't you, Grace?"*

"Sorry," I say, pushing those thoughts away, pasting a wobbly smile on my face. "I shouldn't take up any more of your time."

I walk away, feeling Boone's eyes on me. But I don't turn back, don't want to give him any more reason to doubt my intentions, my alibi, my story. If we're talking about being a sinner or a saint, I know just what side of the coin I am.

I may be innocent in Patrick's homicide, but I am a murderer.

CHAPTER 4

When I first moved to Garden Temple, after my parents died, I was a kid who had just lost everything. Holding a Hello Kitty suitcase and clutching a stuffed squid, I got out of my aunt Sandy's twelve-passenger van, not knowing what to expect.

I was an only child and had grown up in Seattle with my parents, my dad was a math teacher and coach at the local high school and my mom worked for a software company. While I knew Aunt Sandy and Uncle Joseph from stories my mother would tell, we never once visited them and they never had children. I'd ask, at Thanksgiving or Christmas, when kids at school mentioned relatives coming over for family dinners, why our family never joined us.

We would go, as a unit of three, to the family farm my dad inherited in Wenatchee, a few hours from our home. Mom and Dad explained, while we ate our turkey and mashed potatoes at the farm on 611 Cherry Blossom Lane, that spending quality time with the people you loved was better than stuffy get-togethers with family you hardly knew. It was enough for me; when you're young you don't question what you don't understand. So I didn't. I spent summer vacations at tat big white farm house, swimming in the lake and swinging from the apple trees that dotted the orchard, learning quickly that my parents preferred this to ever seeing our only living relatives, my mom's sister Sandy and her husband Joseph.

My parents' will was written when I was a baby, before things must have changed between Sandy and Mom. Sandy was named my legal guardian and without any protest from the state, the lawyers, or her, after my parents passed I was taken to Garden Temple — though no one from the outside would have called it that. Back then it was just a farm in the middle of nowhere. And I was moving in.

When I stepped out of my aunt's van, I didn't think I was coming home. I felt like Dorothy, in the middle of a tornado, desperate to get back to my house.

But that house was gone and this was where I lived now, the big buildings with half-finished siding, exposed plywood and sheetrock revealing shortages in money that even my ten-year-old mind understood. This place was nothing like the charming neighborhood where I'd learned to ride my bike. And while that north Seattle neighborhood had kids playing outside — it was nothing like this.

Here, children were everywhere. Babies crawling in the dust or balanced on the hips of older children. Kids with crossed arms, taking in my every detail as if cataloguing everything I wore. Teenagers who stopped pushing wheelbarrows or carrying wood, looking at me instead. It wasn't with wonder. It was with envy.

I didn't understand what they could possibly be jealous of. I had just lost everything that mattered. But soon enough I realized I still had something they craved.

Attention.

I was the pretty little orphan girl and all the adults wanted to make sure I was okay. Was I hungry, tired? Did I need a shower? Would I like to see my room? Even the men turned their gazes toward me. They never left.

It wasn't until I was much older that I understood why.

Me coming to Garden Temple was like manna from heaven. I was more than the pretty little orphan girl. I was a rich one.

Turns out my inheritance was the windfall they'd been praying for.

* * *

Driving to the library for my shift seems absurd considering the morning I just had, but I need the money. Until I do more of these home parties, I won't have extra cash.

And as awful as it sounds, Patrick's death affects me financially. Worry rises in hot waves as I wonder how I'll be able to continue paying for Ruthie's ballet class now that Patrick isn't here to help me out. He'd insisted, but now thinking of him in monetary values feels wrong.

After I park downtown, I check my phone. I missed three calls from Anna. I didn't cry in front of the officers, even though I nearly did with Boone — but I have a feeling I won't be able to keep my composure with Anna.

Listening to her voicemail sends a wave of nausea through me. She's sobbing, her words broken up, but I can understand the gist. The officers got ahold of her. She knows what happened. She knows her brother is gone. Dead.

I call her back, knowing I'm already cutting it close for making it to work on time. What would life be like if I didn't have to choose between consoling a friend and money? I hate that my life is such a tightrope, but I know it is worth the cost. My daughters need more than Garden Temple could offer.

My son does too.

But as the call goes to voicemail, I put off thoughts of Abel. My son, who doesn't live with me. He is a rabbit trail of regret and I can't get lost down that path right now. I have too many other things to deal with.

"Anna, it's me," I say. "I'm thinking of you. I'm here if you need anything. I get off at four and will try you again on my lunch break. I'm so sorry. So, so sorry."

Hanging up, I feel raindrops begin to fall. I squeeze my eyes shut, not wanting to look into the sky now covered in gray.

* * *

"Mom!" Olive races to the front door as I step inside the house. I drop my tote bag, and she immediately grabs it, looking through the books I brought home. One perk of working at the library is I am able to pick up new books every day.

The girls love to read, something I find miraculous. "Ohhh, this one looks good," Olive says, flipping the cover over and reading the back. "It's a ghost mystery."

Ruthie frowns. "I don't like ghosts." I remember last night, Olive's teasing about something lurking in the basement. I wish I would have remembered earlier and picked something different to bring home.

I ask the girls how school went, hoping they don't ask about my day. I'm not ready to tell them. Before I drove home I spoke with Anna on the phone; she was a wreck, understandably. Patrick's condo is a crime scene. His homicide is all over the news. We made plans for tomorrow morning, before I go to work, and I am hoping by then there will be some answers.

Olive leaves the room to take a shower and I move to the kitchen, opening the pantry and pulling out a box of noodles and a can of diced tomatoes.

"Spaghetti?" Ruthie says, smiling, clutching a Magic School Bus book as she sits on the stool in the kitchen.

"Yep, wanna help?" I ask, not knowing how in the world I am going to explain Patrick's death to them.

Ruthie pops off the stool and opens the fridge, getting out Parmesan cheese and a container of mushrooms.

They adored Patrick. He was one of those guys who could walk into a room and put everyone at ease. He'd remember your name and always gave advice, knew how to hold court with a group of strangers.

He was like Jeremiah in those regards — charismatic, and well-liked. But Patrick wasn't judgmental. He was warm. Inviting. He listened like every word you said was important and he had nowhere else to be but there, giving you his full attention.

Jeremiah on the other hand . . . he was the pastor at Garden Temple and could hold the congregation's attention, but it all came at a price. Complete and absolute submission.

People fell for it because they believed Jeremiah loved them. But he didn't. Doesn't. The only person Jeremiah loves is himself.

"Mom, what happened to this picture?" Ruthie asks, walking over to me at the stove where I've got water boiling.

I turn to her and see the photo of Patrick, Treydon, and me from last month's recruitment banquet is ripped in half.

My spine stiffens as I take it from her —it's the same photo that was smashed on Patrick's mantel.

Just then, Olive walks into the kitchen, tears down her cheeks, a towel wrapped around her body. Her hair's wet, water droplets hitting the hardwood floor. Her eyes are wide, terrified.

"Mom," she says. "I think Dad was in the house."

"What do you mean?" I ask, clutching the halves of the photo.

"It's his favorite." She hands me an empty glass bottle of Coke.

I shake my head, taking the bottle from her hands. "Where was this?"

"In your bedroom, Mom."

I swallow, thinking of Jeremiah being here. In my home. No.

He couldn't have been. Could he?

CHAPTER 5

When I left Garden Temple, it was under the guise of a grocery run.

"I just don't get why you're going today, it's not the first of the month," Lydia said, annoyed with my decision to buck the norm. At twenty-five, she'd been Jeremiah's second wife for ten years and she thought she knew everything.

But she didn't. She still thought Jeremiah was the second coming.

When he'd told me the Revelation, that God had commanded him to take Lydia as his wife, I remember the relief I had felt.

That day I did my best to appear pious. I bowed my head, remaining reverent, but inside I was feeling nothing but joy.

I would no longer be the only woman meant to satisfy Jeremiah at night. The only woman who felt the pain of lying beneath a man who didn't see her as a person, only as a vessel for his progeny.

"I asked her this morning," he'd told me. We were on the back porch where I'd been sitting, watching Olive play in the dirt, rolling a truck back and forth. I was twenty and a mother of two and so tired. My husband was only a decade older than me yet acted as if he were a wise old man.

He wasn't.

"Her parents know?" I had asked, my fingers playing with the edge of my apron, trying to quell my happiness. I would no longer be the only woman bearing the brunt of his rage. His manic moments. His highs that shook the house, his lows that had me walking on eggshells.

"It was their idea."

I pressed my lips together. "I thought it was God's idea."

Jeremiah's eyes met mine, flashing irritation. "You being funny?"

I stood, shaking my head. Not wanting to fight. He took a swig from his bottle of Coke, what he called his one and only vice.

Guess he didn't count smacking me as a vice. That was discipline, he said. I chose to believe him for far too long.

In the kitchen, all those years later, Lydia was making supper, playing the role I was never very good at. Being the doting wife. I tried. Really, really tried. But after Abel was born, my next pregnancy ended in loss; two days after I gave birth to Esther, she died. It changed me. Yes, I had more children, and taught them Bible verses and made bread from scratch and folded laundry. I did all the right things but it wasn't enough. I wasn't enough.

Leaving meant Lydia and Naomi, his third wife, would be there without me to step in, take the hits I knew he meant for them.

Olive was so big then, in the eyes of Garden Temple. I'd heard the whispers, but I'd pushed them away, pretending I'd misunderstood.

But when Jeremiah confirmed the rumors, when he told me the plan for his daughter, I got sick. The joy I felt when he shared the news of his marriage to Lydia, I'd been so happy it hurt. Now, though, I knew better.

I wouldn't wish this hell on anyone.

Certainly not my little girl.

"She will marry Bishop Thomas," he'd told me. Drinking another Coke, sucking the sugary sweet liquid between his two front teeth. I grabbed that bottle from his hand and I threw it against the window, shattering them both, same as my heart.

"No," I shouted. "You aren't doing this."

All the children came running to the yard, the broken glass everywhere, and I leaned over, sick. Vomiting on the dirt. Still, there were no sidewalks, all this time later. Nearly twenty years Garden Temple had been my home and we hadn't gone anywhere. Dirt-covered paths and plywood-covered half-finished houses. Not a home in sight.

I wiped my mouth, lifting my head, and Jeremiah slapped me, hard. Blood in my mouth, tears in my eyes. Bile still rising. And my heart broken so many times there was nothing left to pick up.

I said nothing. I walked into the kitchen and I opened the fridge, taking the bottles of his precious Coke and throwing them out the now smashed window, one after another. The whole family watching. Jeremiah, Lydia and Naomi, and our collective nine children. Disgusted.

Not with him. Not with the man who raised his hand, brought down the hammer same as the blade, slicing through me; he wasn't the sinner. It was me.

I had nowhere to go; still I ran. Through the house, toward the field, down to the creek, and that's where I cried. I couldn't see straight.

Bishop Thomas was thirty-eight years old. Olive was not even thirteen.

I wanted to tell the police. Tell them all the secrets from this place.

But I had secrets too.

One secret, really. And Jeremiah knew it.

It kept me there at Garden Temple. Kept me quiet. Kept me in line.

But where was the line anymore? I just crossed it with each bottle I broke and how do you go back to the beginning when that story has been split in two? My life was a fissure, a before and after; and if this was the after, what was the next part called?

I had no family besides the family here, no one to turn to.

I wiped my eyes, fury rising. I would not let Olive have the same fate as me.

Abel, the son I gave birth to when I was the same age he is now — fifteen — is more his father than me. His eyes so far away they couldn't see me for what I was. Does any teenage boy see his mother as a person?

Still, he was his father's son, through and through, and I'd lost my only boy a long time ago. He looked up to his father the same way he looked down at me and there was no reaching him. At fifteen he was no longer mine to hold.

I washed my face in the cold creek, mosquitos on the surface of the water and I didn't care if they bit me. How could I bleed anymore when all life had already been sucked from my heart? I was left dry. Empty.

But Olive wasn't. No. She was a girl with dark curly hair and a wild freckled face, a smile and eyes that shone. She went to church on Sundays and Mondays and Wednesdays and Thursdays, Fridays too. She went and she prayed and she raised her hands because she believed.

She was alive and well and filled with hope that surpassed all understanding.

I wouldn't let Jeremiah or Garden Temple or Bishop Thomas take that from her.

No.

Because after her it would be Ruthie, my youngest. And then who would be left?

I made a plan. For a month I skimmed cash from the offering plates, stole from the grocery money, took every cent I could find until there was enough for gas, for a week's worth of food. For a motel far enough away that we wouldn't be found.

Then I packed the van with necessities, nothing more.

Lydia stood dicing potatoes for a stew I wouldn't eat. She looked at me with hate, but that was nothing new. Ever since the night of the broken bottles everyone saw me with fresh eyes. Eyes that said you are not worthy of Jeremiah's love.

But I didn't care about that. I only cared about my girls, my boy. I cared about giving them a fighting chance because it was the one and only thing I had to give.

"I ran out of cornmeal," I told Lydia. "I need it for bread."

"Just make some baking powder biscuits."

"Jeremiah's out of his Coca-Cola, too," I said, knowing how the words rattled in my throat. Would she call me on this?

Lydia added a can of tomato paste to the boiling pot as Naomi walked in the kitchen with Jolene, her four-month-old baby on her twenty-year-old hip. "You're going to the store?" she asked, her long blonde hair wrapped in a neat bun on top of her head. She had four babies under five, yet she always looked so damn perfect. How? Why?

I might never know because I was leaving.

"Yes," I told her. "Olive and Ruthie are coming with me."

"Will you get me some pads?" Naomi asked.

"You're already back on your cycle?" Lydia asked, eyes narrowed. Calculating dates. Days. She counted those things as if they would give her a sense of control in a life where she had none.

Naomi's cheeks turned pink. How could she be embarrassed about a period after she gave birth four times?

"I'm pregnant, actually," she said. "I just need panty liners, really."

My heart tugged; wishing I could scoop Naomi up, all her innocence, and protect her from this place. I'd always been closer to her than Lydia, and a few times she had even confided in me when Jeremiah was too rough with her.

Lydia didn't say congratulations. She'd given birth twice, but had been trying again for the last two years. At Garden Temple, giving birth was the only time a woman was seen as a blessing. I understood her longing. She blinked rapidly, tears so close to falling. She pushed them away, turned on her heels, and left the kitchen.

I gave Naomi a hug, the baby clinging to her shirt. I kissed Jolene's head, Naomi's cheek. I wanted to say more. What? Run?

Then it was my turn to leave without another word. Olive and Ruthie were in the yard, and they raced over to me. "Get in the van," I said. "Now."

They were such obedient little girls. They did as I asked, buckling up without question.

When we started driving away, they asked where we were going. I was scared to tell them the truth. Scared they might hate me for tearing them away from the one and only life they ever knew.

But I was more scared of what staying would cost them. I didn't want any more secrets. No more lies.

"Far away," I told them honestly. "And we are never, ever coming back."

CHAPTER 6

I stand with the kids as they wait to get on the school bus. As the year has gone on, I've grown less cautious with the girls. When we first left Garden Temple I walked them to their classroom doors every morning, wanting to see with my own two eyes that they were safe. Eventually I began relaxing on my intensity. The school bus saved time and money, and I didn't have loads of either. And they are smart girls. They'd never get in a stranger's car or skip class.

But now, with Patrick's death — and the gnawing fear that Jeremiah is to blame — I'm reverting to my old patterns. I'm not the only one. Ruthie was clingy last night, insisted on sleeping in my bed — which is something she hasn't asked to do in nearly nine months. The news of Patrick's death rattled her, and I'm sure my anxiety around the evidence of Jeremiah returning only exacerbated those emotions.

When Olive held the empty glass Coke bottle out to me last night at dinner, instead of calmly reacting, I promptly fell apart. Maybe it's bad form for a mother to do this. To cry, without answers. But I don't have any. And they needed to know Patrick was dead. They had the right to that information. After living with so many secrets for so long at Garden

Temple I wasn't about to start a new life by offering them half-truths. They deserved more.

"Patrick is gone," I'd said. "He was killed."

Ruthie had gasped, tears in her eyes. "What?"

I shook my head. "I don't know. But . . ." My eyes had betrayed me. They strayed to the empty bottle on the kitchen counter.

Olive followed my train of thought. "You think Father did this?"

My spine had straightened. I wiped my eyes. Calling it out somehow steeled my resolve. "No, of course not," I said, not wanting to put that sort of heartache on my daughters. "The police are working on it. They will find answers."

Ruthie had wrapped her arms around me, crying. "But Patrick was so nice to us." Her hot tears fell down her cheeks.

"I know, sweetie. I know." Tears fell down mine too.

Olive, though, was bracing to pit herself against me. "Father would never do this. You know why? If he knew where we lived, wouldn't he be coming here to see us? Not hurt your friend?"

"But he did come here, didn't he?" Ruthie asked, stepping away from me and reaching for the Coke bottle. "He came here today."

I grabbed the bottle from her, dropping it in the recycling. Turning to my girls, I implored them. I'd already lost Abel. I couldn't lose them too. "If you see your father . . . run. If he tries to talk to you, scream. Do you understand? Stay together. Always."

"Why would Father hurt Patrick, though?" Ruthie asked.

Olive's eyes flashed with annoyance, but she blinked it away, instead making me her enemy. "Because he probably thought Mom was in love with him."

"Were you, Mommy?" Ruthie asked.

"No, sweetie, I wasn't."

"According to Garden Temple you were sinning. You would go to his home, alone. No chaperone. You're still married to Father. You're a sinner—"

"That's enough," I'd shouted, the palm of my hand flat against the kitchen counter.

Ruthie was crying — not just about Patrick anymore. Abut Olive and me fighting. About her father being called a killer. About not knowing what was right or wrong, true or false. She was eight years old and spent most of that time being fed lies. I was trying to undo so much damage but it hadn't been that long. I was still learning what was true and false myself.

So when she crawled into my bed later that night, I let her. I pulled her close, kissed her soft curls, thanked a God I don't understand that she was here, with me. Olive slept across the hall in her twin bed. She kept the lamp on, the door open. She wanted me to believe she didn't need anyone, anything, but I knew that deep down she was also just a girl who'd grown up being told the world was the enemy.

Today is a new day though, and I push the thoughts of last night away. The bus pulls up and I kiss Ruthie on the cheek, hugging her tight. "Stick together, please."

Olive lifts her eyebrows, smirking.

"I don't want to sit alone," Ruthie says. They attend a K-8 public STEM school. Apparently the spots are coveted. I had no idea when I registered the girls, just grateful they could be in the same building every day, and also, the same bus.

My eyes plead for Olive to soften her hard edges. Olive's shoulders fall, she nods, takes Ruthie's hand. "Colossians 3:20. 'Children, obey your parents in everything, for this pleases the Lord.'" Her small defiance forgotten. Her Garden Temple education shining through — God first, family second, always.

Ruthie's nose scrunches up. "Mom says that—"

I cut her off, not wanting to discuss anything as other mothers watch. Avery and Julia, moms who were at my wELLEness party, are waving goodbye to their own kids as they board the bus.

"Oh, Gray," Avery says, her eyes sympathetic, walking toward me. "How are you? On Facebook I saw a post about Patrick Kelly. You were friends, right?"

My eyebrows lift, and I nod slowly. "Yes, I was the one who called the police." I bite my bottom lip, hating this sort of confrontation — not being on social media means I miss out on news like this.

Patrick had said I needed to make some accounts if I wanted to network, and that I would need to in order to take things to the next level. I'd shrugged it off. "Can't I just do deliveries for you?" I had asked him.

"Not forever," he'd said, wagging a finger. "You need to take things to the next level to support your girls."

He was so good at reminding me of the why behind my decision to sell wELLEness. "Besides, it's easier for women to sell this product than men."

The products in the wELLEness catalogue are predominately catered to women — but there are a growing number of items available that are targeted at a male audience. None of that mattered considering Patrick's sales numbers. Patrick was moving way more multivitamins than anyone else in the region. And considering I've only hosted one home party, I have a lot of learning to do since Patrick is no longer here to teach me.

But that isn't important right now. What matters now is figuring out what Jeremiah was trying to prove by killing Patrick. And how he found us. How long has he been watching us? What's next . . . Would he take my daughters?

"They don't know who the killer is, right?" Julia asks. Avery shoots her a look but I don't let their interest ruffle me. I'm used to women who are in my business. Just now I don't live with them.

I shake my head. "I don't think anyone has been identified. I bet you know more than me, though, since I'm not on social media."

Julia sighs, shaking her head. "Do you need anything? Anything at all?"

"Thanks." I run a hand though my hair. "I'm doing okay, all things considered. I'm actually headed over to the wELLEness offices to talk to the owner. I think she's going to talk about next steps," I say, looking at my garbage and recycling bins at the curb. "I should get going."

"Of course," Avery says. "If you need anything, help with the girls or whatever, give us a holler, okay?"

I wave goodbye, appreciating their respect. They could have asked for grim details about the crime scene. Lydia would have.

I pull my empty garbage cans toward the house, wanting to inch away from the conversation. Last night I rolled them out, knowing Jeremiah's bottle of Coke was going to be taken away. Now, I lift the lids, checking. It's gone.

Exhaling, I tidy the kitchen — loading the breakfast plates in the dishwasher and taking out a pound of ground beef for tacos tonight. Then I grab my keys and purse, heading to the car.

When I pull up to the wELLEness office in downtown Tacoma, I slide nude lipstick on my lips and run a hand through my hair. One of the first things I did when I left Garden Temple was cut straight through my thick braid that felt like a rope. It hung down my back but might as well have been tied around my neck.

I've only been to the headquarters twice. Once with Anna when I'd been with her out running errands, and once with Patrick when I officially signed up as a rep. The place intimidates me. A remodeled building, it's all glass and concrete. The interior of the offices are modern too, like Patrick's condo, but instead of only gray and white furniture, there are pops of bright green everywhere.

It's the opposite of my current home in every way — I do everything in my power to make my little bungalow a cozy haven for the girls. Reupholstering thrifted furniture with discount fabric, using my skills as a homemaker to make the place, well, a home. And nothing about it is sleek. But then again, nothing about me is sleek either.

Which is why Anna and Patrick bringing me into their fold always perplexed me. Whenever I voiced this to them, they looked at me like I was crazy. "But you are so retro,"

Anna would say. "You know how to make kombucha without a recipe. And Elle may own a wellness company, but you can make your own soap. You're like, the original."

Patrick would shrug. "Besides, you're thin, your skin is flawless, and you are the least frazzled mother I've ever met. You play it cool, Gray. You'll sell this product without ever having to open a catalogue."

But I couldn't help feeling like they were seeing a different version of me. I can't ever seem to see the same thing when I look in the mirror.

As I lock the car, I look over my shoulder with the familiar fear of Jeremiah being around the corner. When Anna called me last night, asking me to come in and talk to her and Elle, I agreed, of course. I was at the crime scene — saw what happened firsthand. They deserved the entire story.

But when I step out of the elevator, I see the cops from yesterday are here, too. York, the officer with the pointy nose, and Boone, the detective who looked at me and made me feel like he could see clear through me. It was unnerving.

I bite my bottom lip, adjusting the purse on my shoulder, reminding myself that I'm a grown woman who won't be intimidated by men in power. They're in Patrick's office — it faces the lobby with glass windows, and Boone's eyes rake over me. I swallow, looking away.

I gravitate toward Elle, who stands with crossed arms, watching the officers in Patrick's doorway. They are opening all his drawers, and packing a box with his computer.

"Oh, Gray," Elle says, seeing me. She pulls me into a hug, smelling of Summer-Camp — her new fragrance line that infuses essential oils and nostalgia. This particular blend infuses watermelon and vetiver. Meant to give both clarity and . . . calm? Happiness? I don't know — to be honest the products have begun to blend together.

"Why are the police here?" I ask, my voice low.

Elle rolls her eyes, clearly annoyed. "Anna left a voicemail for Patrick, apparently it was heated. They wanted to ask her some questions."

"Did they finish?"

Elle nods. "Just wrapped up. And now they're looking through his office." Her shoulders fall and she looks to the sky. She's the most sophisticated woman I've ever met. Patrick says she is the PNW version of Gwyneth Paltrow. Elle isn't interested in the trendy jade eggs of L.A., preferring the evergreen forest version, crystal-infused oils featuring cedar and spruce. "Anna's back here."

I walk with Elle through the lobby toward the kitchen. Anna isn't alone, she's with Treydon, and we're clearly interrupting something. Their eyes are both fixed on Anna's phone screen. The moment they see us, she drops it in the pocket of her jean jacket.

"You know Treydon, don't you?" Elle asks me. "He's my assistant. Or he was until Danny poached him."

"We've met," I say softly. Anna's been crying, Treydon looks like he hasn't slept. And even Elle seems less polished than normal.

"Oh Gray," Anna says, wrapping me in a hug. "It's all so much. You've been through hell, finding him like you did . . ." She shakes her head, wiping away tears.

I don't want this to be about me. "Your brother is gone, how are *you*?"

"A mess. I have high blood pressure and my heart has been racing all day. I'm a wreck, Gray. I can't imagine life without him. Jasper is talking with a lawyer. Someone murdered him! Nothing feels right."

"It probably won't for quite a while," I say. "But I'm glad your husband is speaking with a lawyer." Turning to Treydon, I ask how he's holding up. My mind flashes to the photo on Patrick's mantel. Him, Patrick and me, glass smashed. The one on my fridge, ripped in two.

"A wreck," he says. "Who would do this?"

Not having an answer I can admit to, I sit in a chair at the table.

Treydon keeps speaking. "What's worse is I hadn't seen him all week. I never got to say goodbye."

I frown. Remembering the text from Patrick the night of my party — why he cancelled. Treydon and Anna messed up an order, they were with him. Something feels off.

"What about you, Anna?" I ask. "When had you seen him last?"

Before she can answer, the officers enter. A third cop, Truce, is here now, too. "We need to search your office now," he tells Elle.

"This is all totally unnecessary," Elle says, running a hand through her hair.

York smirks. "Why don't you want us to look? You got something to hide?"

She scoffs. "How dare you."

"We have the warrant, which we presented upon arrival," Boone says dryly. "At this point, how you feel isn't exactly relevant."

I stand, not wanting to be here while the police are looking around, asking questions. I have reasons to keep my head down and I'm not about to give them a reason to look me in the eyes.

"There's a lot going on here," I say. "Why don't we catch up later?" Treydon, Elle and Anna nod, understanding. "And if there's anything you need, let me know."

I walk through the hall quickly, feeling less like myself every second I'm here in this polished space. I want out of the glass offices and concrete floors. The elevator takes me to the bottom level. I step out, wanting sunshine and solid ground and — someone takes hold of my arm.

I gasp, feeling a hand clasp around my arm, and I see a flash of my husband. Of Jeremiah.

I blink, realizing the grip is softer. Not intending to hurt, but rather to get my attention. I turn. It's not Jeremiah at all. It's Detective Boone.

CHAPTER 7

The parking garage is filled with cars, but there are no other people in sight. It's just Boone and me. I stare at his hand on mine, and he pulls it back quickly.

"I was calling your name," he says.

Frowning, I pull the keys from my pocket. I must have been lost in thought. "I didn't hear you."

"Really?" He clears his throat, and I look away. Wanting to get away. From him. This moment. The last thing I want is to be alone with a detective.

"Sorry, what did you need?" I ask, trying to recover. He is giving me a quizzical look of disbelief.

"I had some questions for you," he says. "Do you have a few minutes?"

I press my lips together. "It's early release day at my daughters' school," I explain. "I want to get home."

"I'll just follow you, then," he says, not waiting for a reply. He simply walks away, to an old red Jeep Cherokee, and gets in.

I get in my sedan and pull out of the garage, irritated that Boone is doing what he wants. But isn't that all men? They get to decide what kind of life they want, and then they go lead it.

I pull onto the street, rolling down my windows — suddenly feeling stifled — and check my rearview mirror. Boone is on my tail. My house is only a few miles away, and when I park my car in front of my home, he's still on my heels. I dig in my purse for Anxiet-EZ, wELLEness's all-natural anxiety relief pills made with valerian and lemon balm.

"What's that?" Boone asks, looking through my open window. I hold up the bottle. He takes it from me, reading the label. "This is all bullshit, you realize that, right?"

I reach for the bottle, stuffing it back in my purse, then roll up the windows. He watches me, pulling back before I pinch his fingers.

He follows me up to the house. "So, you didn't know Patrick all that long, did you?"

I shake my head. "No. I just met Anna and Patrick this fall."

"Got pretty close pretty fast, huh?"

Unlocking my front door, I narrow my eyes. I can see straight through the foyer into the kitchen, and the back door is open. Without hesitating, I march through the house, on high alert. Did Jeremiah come back here? Why? It's so careless . . . unless he wants to be caught.

"Uh, what is it?" Boone asks, on my heels. I didn't invite him in, but maybe the faster we get this over with, the sooner he'll be done with me. The last thing I want is to have a detective looking deeper into my life than necessary.

At the back door, I slowly turn the handle, closing it. Then I press my back to the door, looking around my kitchen. I cleaned it this morning before I left, and nothing is amiss. Except for the open door. No way would I have left it like that.

Then, on the counter, I notice another half-empty bottle of Coke. Stepping toward it, I pick it up, turning it in my hand. What I'm looking for, I don't know. I just know it wasn't here when I left.

I close my eyes, breathing through my nose. What is Jeremiah trying to tell me?

Boone is watching me, closely. "What is it?" he asks again.

"Nothing." My voice is tight, betraying my feigned nonchalance. "It's nothing." I set the bottle down and turn to him. He's walking out of my kitchen, into the living room. Looking around, as if searching for clues.

I try to see this house through his eyes. The handmade quilt on the threadbare sofa. The open notebook of mine, with a meal plan and a grocery list laid out. The random stack of books on the coffee table, the ones I read every night. Books on the solar system and the Revolutionary War and poetry. Desperate to fill in the gaps of my education.

He is seeing a room pieced together with all that I've got. My assets. My hopes, my dreams. I can cook and I can sew and I can read. I'm trying. So hard. But as Boone looks around the room, I feel seen in a way I didn't when the moms from the neighborhood were over the other night. They saw my little life as charming. Boone, though, is a detective. And every little thing he notices is a clue. I don't want him to see anymore.

"What sorts of questions did you have?" I ask from the kitchen, not even wanting to set foot in the same room with him. I want him gone.

He joins me in the kitchen. "I wanted to tell you that you're no longer a suspect."

"Had I been a suspect?" I ask. When he doesn't answer right away, I ask if he wants something to drink, feeling parched myself.

He eyes the counter. "I'd take a Coke."

I swallow, eyes darting to the half-empty bottle. "Oh, we don't have any."

He lifts his eyebrows, but doesn't question me. "Water's fine."

I walk to the cabinet and pull out two water glasses, filling them at the sink. Boone and I sit at the kitchen table, and I take a long drink, watching him watch me.

He looks ridiculous in that thrifted chair. I found this table and chair set at a thrift store, and sanded it, then painted it white. Using sandpaper, I wore down the edges of the furniture, making it look shabby chic. A style that's outdated according to Anna — but it feels homey. It feels like me.

But Boone is a broad-shouldered man, and he looks like he's playing Goldilocks and the Three Bears, sitting in someone else's seat.

"You were a suspect until we confirmed your alibi."

"I had a home party the night he died. But he had texted me before it started," I explain.

"And what was he texting about?"

I consider lying . . . but I know he could access my phone records if he wanted. I have no power with him. "He told me that Treydon and Anna were over at his house, and that there had been a problem. He had planned to come over and help me with the party that night."

"Did you and Patrick spend a lot of time together?" Boone asks.

I shrug, looking at the clock on the oven. The girls won't be home for half an hour. "We saw one another a few times a week. He helped me get started with wELLEness, and he was my up-line."

"What's an up-line?"

"Simply put, he was a step up the line from me. Everyone has an up-line in the company, it's your point of contact. Except the owner, Elle, of course."

"So it was strictly a business relationship?" Boone asks. I know what he's getting at.

"Patrick was very friendly to me. He and Anna both. They welcomed me into their lives. They helped me get this house, we had dinner together every week — they are, were, my closest friends."

"How did you meet exactly? You said at work?"

I nod. "I told you, I work at the library. Anna was in, looking for a book, and we started talking. She was looking for a recipe. For kombucha. I've made it, and we got to talking. Anna mentioned some essential oils, and I knew their uses — we had things in common. Both of us are into all-natural products, and it's why we became friends."

Boone pulls out a small notepad from his suit jacket pocket, and a pen. He uncaps it, bouncing it on the paper. "And Patrick?"

"I was helping Patrick deliver his wELLEness products to clients; so maybe we started out as colleagues but we quickly became friends. He was helping me grow this business into a supplemental income."

Boone sits back in his chair. "And you wanted that? Two random people quickly becoming involved in your life? Don't you have other friends who you could have dinner with?"

I bite my bottom lip. How to explain to a detective that you are on the run? That you've been a cult member for twenty years and were complicit in things that in your heart you knew were wrong? How do you say, I stayed as long as I did because I was scared? How do you say, I'm still scared now?

I'm scared Jeremiah might find me — that he already has. I'm scared he'll take my daughters, scared he'll use the fact that I killed a man to ruin me.

I'm afraid that the careful world I've built will fall apart.

If I open up the story book of my past, there will not be a happy ending. That was taken from me a long time ago.

I can't lead with the truth. And I can't lead with my heart. So where does that leave me?

When I was younger, Jeremiah used to say I was too soft with the kids. And my sister wives always said I was too emotional with my reactions. So I started to bottle everything up.

And then I escaped to the real world, and it just got worse. More terrifying to let down my guard. I had to be vigilant if I wanted my girls to be safe. If I wanted us to survive.

Now, though, I look at Boone and I wonder what it would be like to let some of that guard down, to let someone in — really in. He is looking at me like he wants to know it all, and with his rumpled shirt and way-past-five o'clock shadow, the stress lines around his eyes, I have a feeling he has some demons of his own.

"Do you ever meet someone and feel like they are the lifeline you've been looking for?" I ask Boone.

He bristles, his gaze on mine. Like I've just hit the nail on the head and it hurts, the piercing point of the iron on wood.

"Patrick and Anna, they were your lifeline?" He asks it as if he already knows the answer.

"Yes," I tell him, not wanting to look into his eyes. "That's exactly what they were to me. I was recently out of a relationship, and they helped me get on my feet."

"And were you and Patrick romantically involved?"

I shake my head softly. "Patrick liked me, but he liked everyone. He was a charismatic person, charming and generous. We spent time together, alone. Went on walks beside the water by his condo, and he was really good with the girls."

"You have more than one daughter?" Boone asks.

I nod. "Yeah, Olive and Ruthie. How about you?" I look at his bare ring finger, but know it doesn't mean anything. I don't wear a wedding band.

"No, I don't have any children." Boone clears his throat, as if he wants to change the subject. "And do you have any idea who may have wanted Patrick dead?"

"I've been thinking about it ever since I found him . . . and I can't think of anything. Anyone. I know that isn't helpful. He wasn't the sort of person to have enemies."

"And his sister Anna, what about her?"

"What about her? She has the perfect life."

"What do you mean by that?" Boone presses.

"I mean she has an adoring husband, Jasper, a supportive brother. A gorgeous home. She's the sort of person who has their whole life sorted."

"And she was the one who looped you into this MLM?"

I frown. "What do you mean, looped?"

"Multi-level marketing is a glorified pyramid scheme, and she saw someone who was lonely and drew you in to her web. And her brother Patrick seems to have benefitted from her networking."

I balk at this summary. "You're wrong on all accounts. I wasn't tricked into a pyramid scheme. The products wELLE-ness offers are incredible. They are life enhancing. They work."

The corner of Boone's mouth goes up, like he thinks I'm a joke. "A true believer, huh?"

The front door opens, and Ruthie and Olive bound into the kitchen. They slow when they see Boone. Their childhood at the compound trained them to remain quiet, not to ask questions of those in authority. And as they take in his police badge, I watch the wheels in their minds turning. But still, they look to their shoes, not speaking.

"These your girls?" he asks, getting up from the kitchen chair, thankfully dropping the conversation.

"Yes, Olive is twelve and Ruthie is eight." I stand too, and pull Ruthie into a hug, kissing the top of her hair. "I'm guessing you two are hungry? Why don't you go put your backpacks in your rooms first?"

The girls nod, and leave with small smiles, not saying a word to him. I hate how they've been taught to keep quiet. One year is not long enough to rewire their brains. We need more time. I can't let Jeremiah come for them.

Boone gives me a tight smile. "I'll leave you to it, Gray." I walk him to the front door, opening it for him. "And you know, if someone is entering your home without your permission, that's a crime."

"What are you talking about?" I shake my head, pretending I don't know what he's referring to.

"I'm a detective, Gray. It's my job to know when someone isn't telling the truth."

"I didn't kill Patrick," I say with a sharp, hushed voice.

Boone smirks. "I know that. But you are hiding something."

CHAPTER 8

I close the door on Boone, rattled by his words. All of them. Not just that he knows I am hiding something, but the way he broke down my relationships with Anna and Patrick so quickly.

I can't believe his assessment — mostly because I truly do believe in the products. It's the main reason I decided to join the company. In Garden Temple we rarely went to the hospital. Not even for childbirth. We had a midwife, and we used alternative medicine to treat all our symptoms. Dandelion for constipation and mint for a headache and sunflower to reduce fever.

So when Anna explained the products to me, I was excited. I'd spent my twenties treating sore throats with echinacea, so when she showed me the Echina-Tea, I was sold. Without the massive herbal garden we had at Garden Temple, this felt like an easy way to access the medicine I was familiar with. The bonus was that I got everything at a discount while I worked for Patrick and began building my own client base.

I like working at the library — I crave quiet, calm, order. But the ceiling is low in terms of pay. If I want to live beyond paycheck to paycheck, I would need to make more money.

Anna and Patrick understood that. They wanted me to succeed at this, and they cared for the girls and for me.

But now Boone's words ring loud in my ears, forcing me to reconsider their sincerity in our relationship.

"Mom, can we watch a movie with popcorn?" Olive asks as I reenter the kitchen.

"A movie? It's not even three in the afternoon."

"A documentary then?" she negotiates.

Ruthie is pouring them juice, spilling on the counter. I come up beside her and hold the cup still, helping her.

"Let's see what the options are," I say, giving in. Olive has our family laptop out already and is scrolling through Netflix. Films on Waco, Orthodox Jews, and Rajneeshpuram flit past.

"How about something about nature?" I suggest, not wanting my girls to see anything dark and disturbing by accident. "Or endangered animals?"

They settle on a film about panda bears and I put a pot on the stove to make them popcorn, unsettled by everything the day has offered. As the kernels pop, my eyes land on the back door, the way it was open when I came home. A shiver runs down my spine, to my toes. Grounding me in the reality of this situation. Could Jeremiah really have been here? My mouth goes dry, the sugar-coated Coke bottle leaving a bitter taste in my mouth. I need answers.

Once they have a big buttered bowl between them on the couch, I tell them I need to make some calls in my bedroom.

I climb the stairs to the second floor, where the bedrooms are located, and I exhale, alone for the first time in hours. I pick up Olive's shoes and place them in her room, and grab Ruthie's stuffed pig and place it on her bed. I don't begrudge the girls their misplaced things. Maybe it's because deep down I'm too soft, like Jeremiah assessed. But I know the real reason. It's because they spent their childhoods programmed to believe the world was only black and white, right and wrong, good and bad — and I don't want them to think that way anymore. Leaving a mess in the hallway doesn't deserve consequences, just like being moody when the day hasn't gone well doesn't justify a slap to the face. It's too late for Abel to learn about grace, but it isn't too late for my daughters.

I sit on my bed, scared but desperate. I need to make this call. I pull out my phone, dialing the number to the house at Garden Temple. We had one phone, hooked up to a landline, and I know at this time in the afternoon, Jeremiah will be out working in his office at the church, and that Lydia will be at the schoolhouse with the older kids, leaving Naomi home alone.

If someone else picks up, or she doesn't answer, I can hang up. But if she does . . . I might get some answers I need.

"Hello?" Naomi's wispy voice asks.

I know this phone can't be traced — but still, I haven't called Garden Temple once since I left a year ago.

"Naomi?" I say, my voice catching. I remind myself this is not the time to be soft, I must be strong. "It's me, Grace."

"Oh my heart," she whispers. "Grace, where are you?"

"Are you alone?" I ask.

"Just with Jolene and Sadie. I had another girl," she says, brushing past all the questions she must have about where I am. Why I left. Then again, maybe she understands perfectly well. "She's three months. And a terrible sleeper. Just like Johnathon."

Her oldest is Johnathon, five now. Five kids, five and under, and she's just twenty-one.

"I miss you," I tell her, words I wasn't expecting to say. But they're true. Naomi is family. Her children are my children's half-siblings.

Olive would hate me if she knew I was making this call. She'd be jealous. Naomi was her mother too.

"You messed everything up when you left," she says, her voice stretched thin. "Jeremiah was so mad. He took it out on us."

"I'm sorry." And I am. Sorry for the pain my choice inflicted on her. But I'm not sorry for leaving.

"You're so selfish." Naomi sighs. "I'm supposed to hate you, you know that?"

"And do you?" I ask, my voice cracking under the weight of her words.

"You didn't even say goodbye."

"I couldn't risk it."

"Why are you calling now?" she asks, a baby crying close to the receiver. I can imagine her finding a chair in the kitchen, unbuttoning her blouse, offering her newborn her breast. My own chest tightens, lets down. Muscle memory in the worst way.

"I think Jeremiah found us," I tell her. "I think he was just here. Yesterday, and again today."

"Are you close by us?" she asks.

"No, I'm nowhere nearby." It's vague enough that it doesn't give a trail to my doorstep.

"Then he hasn't. He's been here all week."

"You're sure?"

Her sharp laugh snaps me back to reality. I have no real reason to trust that Naomi is on my side. "I know my husband," she says. "And I know where he sleeps."

"But—"

"This is a bad idea, you calling. I don't want to be drawn into any of this." Her words are final, but I can't let this be the end.

"Are you sure he couldn't have travelled across state lines and still been in your bed at night?" I need to know if he could do an eight-hour round trip, and get away with it. But I can't be too direct with my questions — I want to trust Naomi, but I can't. She loves Jeremiah, and her loyalty lies with him.

Her voice is tight. "It's been busy here. We've been holding a revival every night this week, praying for deliverance, mostly, from the world. The world where you live. You're a sinner, Grace. And me talking to you . . . it's wrong."

I want to argue, but I know it's futile. Instead, I direct the conversation back to our husband. "And Jeremiah has been at all these rallies?"

Naomi sighs. "Not all of them. He's been busy too, preoccupied with his choices. He's picking a bride."

My skin turns cold. "He's marrying again."

I know lovesick Jeremiah. He says it's all about God's plan, but I know Jeremiah finds pleasure in sharing his bed with new, younger women. I stood by and watched him do it twice. Now he is doing it again. Bile rises in my throat as I try to push down the memories — watching Naomi walk down the aisle in a white dress Lydia and I had sewn for her, toward our husband. I remember how young she looked, so small, so fragile. In the end, I was the one who was too broken to stay, my heart made of glass. I couldn't tough it out anymore.

"Who is he marrying?"

Naomi is silent and I fear I pushed her too far over the edge, that she's gone. But then her voice cracks and my own eyes fill with tears. Whoever he is marrying, it's going to be hard for Naomi to stand by and watch. For five years she's been his princess, the jewel. Now her crown is being taken.

"I don't know yet. There is talk of several girls. But it will be blessed, no matter. Whoever it ends up being, it's God's plan, right?"

"You don't want me to answer that."

"What happened to you, Grace?" she asks me.

"It was Olive," I say, my words sounding small in light of the fact that Naomi is still there at Garden Temple. Still believing.

"But you always knew Olive would get married one day. It's a part of the plan, the marriage bed is the holiest place and she would have had the prophet's blessing." Naomi sighs. "Jeremiah is the holiest man on earth, and he was the one choosing marriage for his daughter. I don't understand how you could turn your back on God's promises."

"It's not as simple as that."

"It's because you spent ten years in the world, isn't it? That's what Jeremiah says."

"What else does he say?"

"He says that you ran away because evil was embedded in your soul. You had spent too much time with the world to truly understand God's will."

"When does he talk like that, about me?"

Naomi scoffs. "Every night at dinner. It's a part of his reprimand after prayer. Says you are linked to him by marriage and nothing can sever that bond. That one day you will return. He's ordained it, Grace."

I consider that — he is still thinking of me. He hasn't forgotten me by a long shot. He plans on bringing me back one way or another.

"It's all just so sad, Grace," Naomi says. "You always were the righteous one."

I exhale. "No, Naomi. I was just really good at pretending."

CHAPTER 9

After the call with Naomi, everything feels unsettled. Memories of my past have surfaced and I need out of the house. It's cold out though, the dreary February weather making a walk less than enticing.

Wanting to check on the girls and their nature documentary, I walk downstairs, eyeing the defrosted ground beef for dinner, then looking at the clock. It's only one in the afternoon. Early release day means we have a long stretch before it's time to make tacos.

My phone buzzes in my hand, and I look at the text — it's from my neighbor Julia.

> Julia: *I'm having a spontaneous get-together at my place in half an hour. Kids can decorate cookies for Valentine's Day and us mommies can have happy hour. You in?*

I read the text several times. I've never been to Julia's house, but she's only a few doors down, and it will help the afternoon pass quickly. Besides, being here, not knowing if Jeremiah is lurking around the corner, makes me want to run.

> Me: *Sure. I'll bring sprinkles.*

Besides Anna and Patrick, I don't have connections in this city, I don't have friends. Not from work, and not from the girls' school — I keep a low profile for a reason. But I knew when I started selling wELLEness that I would need to broaden my social circle. Ladies from the neighborhood seem the safest way to do that.

Besides, if someone is trying to hurt me and my daughters, having people looking out for me will be a good thing.

As the video wraps up, I tell Ruthie and Olive the plans. Immediately Ruthie brightens. "We get to play at Cleo's house?"

I nod. "Yep, so go brush your hair and put on your jackets."

They smile, excited about decorating cookies, and I root around the cupboard for sprinkles. I had bought pink hearts on impulse last week. Once found, I hand them to Ruthie. "Can you carry these?"

She smiles, taking my hand as we leave the house, bundled up in our coats and boots, the sidewalks wet from the afternoon rain. Olive asks who else is coming.

"Not sure," I say. "But can you please try and be nice?"

"When am I not nice?" she asks, smirking.

"You know what I mean," I say gently. "No judging."

She bites her lip, nodding. Obeying. Olive's teachers say she has a low tolerance for behavior that she deems "inappropriate". She's called classmates sinners and heathens. When she hears other students swearing or cheating on tests or talking about a teacher, she tells them she is praying for them. And she does. At home, she has a journal where she writes down the names of the people she is praying for, and I hear her at night, see her kneeling at her bed. Believing this is the answer. The way toward peace.

But it also means she isn't exactly making friends. Her world is black and white. She's like her brother, only her loyalty lies with me. Abel's lies with his dad. But I didn't give either of them a choice. I didn't ask Abel to run away with me, and I didn't ask Olive if she wanted to stay.

At the front door of Julia's, Ruthie knocks gleefully. Her long brown hair is in two braids, her freckled face grinning, she is the epitome of pure love — not a single corner jaded.

I long to be like her, or to at least hold her child-like innocence in my hands and breathe it in.

I remember being Ruthie's age, before my parents' death, and can imagine myself standing at the neighbor's door, sprinkles in hand. Ready for hot cocoa and laughter and sugar cookies. I can remember the smell of fresh-from-the-oven joy. How simple it was to go to a friend's house and play the day away. It's never been so easy for Ruthie.

Now it feels like make-believe, to be invited into Julia's renovated bungalow; I hear people inside, children shrieking happily, women laughing. I push down the butterflies in my stomach, not wanting to be nervous over what everyone inside this house would deem as so regular.

Julia opens the door, her ponytail swishing, her pink athletic leggings matching the mood. Happy. "You came!"

Ruthie proudly presents the bottle of sprinkles.

"Look at these hearts. Come see the cookies, girls, we have quite the decoration station."

We follow her, and I pull the front door shut. We slip off our jackets and shoes, seeing the pile in the hallway, and I try not to compare myself as we wind our way toward the kitchen. It's all so new, shiny appliances and thick white trim on each window well, a marble island six feet long. What did she think at my wELLEness party? Pity for my thrift store furniture?

It doesn't matter. We're here to have fun, and so I warmly greet the other ladies I know. Kendall is here with her three kids, her youngest, Gordie, sleeping in a Pack n' Play in the corner. And Luna introduces me to her teenage daughter Sophie.

"I thought I could help wrangle the kids," she says with a smile. At fifteen she looks just like her mother, long and lean, graceful, and when Luna mentions her ballet practice later this evening, I nod, not surprised.

"Avery said coming would be more work than it was worth," Julia tells me, handing me a steaming mug. "Those twins keep her so busy," she says with a sympathetic smile.

I take a sip of the drink, eyes widening as I do. It's delicious. "What is this?"

Julia smiles. "Hot buttered rum."

"Oh, I've never had it before. It's really good."

"Thanks. It's worth the calories, right?" Kendall says, bumping my hip as she walks to the kitchen table where the kids are standing with Sophie, bags of icing in hand, containers of different colored frosting and cups of sprinkles everywhere. There must be a hundred heart-shaped cookies baked. They cover every counter in the kitchen.

"You must have been baking these for days," I say, one eye on my girls as they find their way with the other kids at the table. Ruthie and Cleo laugh as they cover their hearts in pink sugar, then lick their fingers the way only third grade girls can. Totally uninhibited. Olive is taking it slower, finding a clean butter knife and evenly spreading white frosting over a cookie.

"Oh, I totally cheated," Julia says. "I just rolled out premade dough."

"Well, they taste good," Kendall says, snapping an undecorated one in half and dunking it in her mug. "I don't bake, though. Can you believe I've never even made a pie?"

Luna laughs. "I'm with you, I can handle cooking. Dinner isn't exactly award-winning at our house, but it's decent. But I've never put in the time to learn to bake."

The women look to me to say something, and I shrug. "Actually, I like baking more than cooking. Especially for holidays."

"I'm not surprised," Julia says. "Your house is so adorable. The other night when we were over, I came home jealous of your handmade decor, so artistic. Me? I just wander Target and buy everything Joanna Gaines."

Luna laughs. "Same. Though I'm partial to Home Goods. They always have the best clearance."

An easy smile fills my face, and the tension in my shoulders fades, the warmth from the rum easing my tension, and I realize these women weren't judging me and my home. They are taking me at face value, welcoming me into their circle.

"Let's sit in the living room," Luna suggests. "Sophie, you got the kiddos?"

Her teenage daughter nods, wiping at a streak of red frosting on Kendall's daughter's cheek. "Sure thing. But I don't think any of us need dinner. We're eating as many as we're decorating."

In the living room, Julia sets a plate of cookies on the coffee table and refills our mugs. As we settle in dark leather sofas, Kendall picks up on a conversation they were having before I got here. "The thing is," she moans. "I didn't think Audrey would go snooping around my nightstand. Where am I supposed to hide my vibrator? A safe?"

Luna laughs. "Oh God, Sophie never found my unmentionables when she was little, but we had a super awkward conversation a few months back where she asked me, point blank, about the first time I had sex." Luna sighs. "I'm not a prude, and she is fifteen, but like, she wanted details. And I just . . ." She shakes her head. "I was unprepared to give them."

I twist my lips, knowing this is totally unchartered territory for me, and the exact reason why I don't get into cozy conversations with other moms. Anna was different, we never spent time on motherhood or relationships — with us it was always about business. About wELLEness . . . and as Julia begins telling the story of her first time having sex, I hear the words *back of a pickup truck* and choose to I drown her out.

Instead of thinking about my first time having sex, my mind instead returns to Boone's words at my kitchen table. *Multi-level marketing is a glorified pyramid scheme, and she saw someone who was lonely and drew you in to her web.*

Was that what it was about? Because it wasn't about gossip, or about the day-to-day dramas we faced as moms. It was only ever about wELLEness.

"What about you, Gray?" Kendall asks.

"Oh, sorry, missed the question."

Kendall walks to the Pack n' Play, lifting out her son, who is now awake. She lifts her top, offering him milk, and she repeats herself. "When was your first time?"

I swallow, remembering. And even though it is out of character I find myself drawn into the moment, to the three women around me. It's a wintery afternoon with an overcast sky, making the moment feel intimate and safe. Offering a sense of security I crave.

"I was fifteen," I tell them, thinking of Jeremiah. Of our wedding night. Of how in the beginning, being with him felt like I was a prize peach, the perfect apple, the only cherry on the tree. It wasn't all bad, being his wife. At first, it felt like I was chosen. It felt like I was his.

"And we were nervous . . ." I lick my lips, wanting to be honest with the story I've never told a single person. "But also giddy. He didn't know what he was doing either, but we were in love. So in love. You know that feeling, where everything seems perfect?"

The women nod knowingly. And so I keep talking. Maybe it's the rum, but maybe not. Maybe I've been wanting someone to ask me my story more than I knew.

"Please tell me you weren't in a truck like me," Julia moans.

"Or a dorm room bunkbed," Kendall snorts.

"No, it was his room," I say, not adding that it was the room shared, the apartment in the back of the church he built. "His bed. It was night, and it was summer. And it was . . . really . . . good." I feel heat rise to my cheeks, surprising myself at the memory. I had been so innocent then, naive. I should have known better. But no one taught me to think for myself. That is why I took Olive away. Why she's never going back.

"Good?" Luna laughs. "Most people's first time is awful, you realize this, don't you?"

"Sorry," I say, lifting my shoulders in a shrug. My confession like a stream valve, a release that I needed in a way

I didn't know. "But it was. And we were like bunnies. We moved from the bed to the floor, and couldn't stop ourselves. The next day I discovered I had rug burn on my knees."

They all crack up, and my cheeks are hot.

"I can't believe I just told you that."

What would they think if they knew that I'd been fifteen, married to a man eight years older than me? They wouldn't be laughing. Not if they knew that in the months after my honeymoon phase, I realized that Jeremiah didn't love me. He'd tricked me. Tricked everyone.

"Oh my God, no, that story is amazing," Kendall says. "Please tell me he didn't break your heart."

"Sadly," I say, shaking my head, a smile still on my face, a pasted-on smile hiding the pain. "Young love never lasts."

Luna leans in, her feet tucked up under her on the couch, her voice low. "I hope Sophie gets something like that. Something tender."

I understand the longing of this mother, wishing to make the world perfect for her child, the one who isn't so little anymore. Abel, also fifteen, is grown in ways I wish he wasn't.

Pressing my lips together, I hope Sophie's first time is nothing like mine. Mine may have been laced with innocence, but it wasn't all sweet. Back then I saw Jeremiah as my savior, now I see him for what he really is. And it got worse from there. Jeremiah offering me as gift to Bishop Micah, his closest friend. A night that burns with pain.

I shove the thought away, pick up a cookie, breaking it in half. A broken heart, held in my hands. I shove a piece in my mouth, wishing I could swallow it whole.

CHAPTER 10

The cookie party was good for a few reasons. Most importantly, it gave me insight into my neighbors' lives. I now know that Julia's husband has a black belt, that Kendall's mother-in-law is in the state Senate, that Luna's brother is a local firefighter. And that Avery's marriage is on the rocks.

I don't know how this information will help me, exactly, but having connections never hurts. I learned that years ago at Garden Temple. Being married to the leader gave me privileges I wouldn't have otherwise had, and gave me leverage. Anyone who befriended me had an instant leg up.

In the two days since the afternoon with my neighbors, I've expected the other shoe to drop. For Jeremiah to be here at the house when I get off work, as I tuck the girls into bed. And the fear that keeps rattling around my mind is, what will I do if he does? I have no way to protect myself besides running.

I saved Detective Boone's number in my phone, and every time it rings I half expect it to be him. With new insight on the case, with a suspect — or with a finger pointed at my husband. But when it finally rings, it isn't Boone. It's Anna.

"There's a party scheduled for tonight at the marina. Can you cover it?" she asks me.

"A party?" I swear I hear her wrong. I'm pulling clothes out of the dryer and think maybe the reception is too shoddy in the basement. As I climb the stairs to the ground floor with the laundry basket in hand, I repeat myself. "A wELLEness party?"

"Yeah," Anna sighs. "I know the timing is crap, but this is with Patrick's VIP customers. And they are all emailing and texting, wanting to be sure they have their products. And you'll be their new rep so it's better to meet with them and make sure they are happy."

"That's a little insensitive, isn't it? Patrick just . . ."

"I know, but they aren't calling me," Anna clarifies. "They're calling corporate. It's just getting down the pipeline to me, and now, to you."

"I see." I put the phone on speaker and begin folding shirts and blue jeans. "Why me? I've only hosted one party."

"This isn't a party per se. The clients are waiting for product that Patrick was supposed to deliver, and they want to reorder. And I'm sure they'll have some questions about the new product line. We want them to feel special, valued."

"But Patrick died three days ago."

"Four."

"What?" I sit down on the couch, trying to understand Anna. Her brother was murdered this week and the count of days feels irrelevant.

"It's been four days and there are no leads and it feels like it could be a long time before anything comes to light. In the meantime, wELLEness is all about self-care, and we all need that right now more than ever. So if Patrick's closest clients are struggling and want to reach out, we should meet them where they are."

"Okay," I say, struggling to understand her logic but not wanting to argue. I know everyone grieves differently and who am I to judge if these customers need some extra doses of Mood-Me to get them through? "Can you text me the details?"

"Of course. It's tonight at seven. I'd go, but it doesn't seem appropriate and I trust you, Gray. So did Patrick."

I end the call feeling torn. On one hand I would do anything to help Anna after all she has done for me the past several months, but on the other, much more logistical hand — I can't leave the girls here. I could bring them, of course, but it doesn't sit right with me.

The other day Luna texted me her daughter Sophie's number, and she was so helpful with the kids at the cookie party. So I reach out to her with a text, surprising myself as I do. But also knowing there is no way I can leave the girls in my house alone with Jeremiah potentially on the loose.

Thankfully Luna has no problem with Sophie watching the girls at their home. "It'll be good for them anyways," Luna says. "To be familiar with another house in the neighborhood."

Later, when I drop them off, I take an extra few minutes in Luna's kitchen, getting a feel for the household, wanting to be sure my girls feel safe here. Ruthie is excited, but she is excited about everything these days and she seems to think Sophie is the most wonderful teenager on the planet, mostly because of her bright purple nail polish. And Olive, miraculously, is immediately won over by the fact they have a piano in the living room.

"Can I play?" she asks Luna.

"Of course, dear. Sophie stopped playing years ago. I'm sure it's out of tune."

Olive sits on the piano bench, back straight. She looks over at me, giving me a soft smile, and my heart beats hard. I haven't heard her play since we fled.

Her fingers dance over the keys as she plays "How Great Thou Art," a classic hymnal. It's beautiful and delicate and a hush falls over the room as we watch her, transfixed. When she finishes, Luna claps. "Bravo! You have such talent, darling."

Olive shrugs. But Luna refuses to dismiss it. "Anytime you want to practice, come over. I work from home so it's no bother. I promise."

When I leave the house, the sense of fear I usually feel has faded. It feels good to know my daughters are in good, capable hands. And so, by the time I arrive at the marina, I feel a much-needed sense of calm. The map on my phone tells me where to turn and soon I am in front of a gorgeous estate on the hill overlooking Puget Sound. There's a gated entrance with a large circular drive, and as I park my modest car I take in the luxury vehicles around me. It makes sense. These are Patrick's VIP clients, and he drove a Tesla for goodness' sake. The amount of wealth in this driveway alone takes my breath away.

But I refuse to let it make me feel small. I open my trunk and pull out the large tote bins filled with the product they ordered. I have done a lot of deliveries for Patrick over the last two months, but never to his most important clients — he handled them. Which I completely understand. He wanted to nurture those relationships since they are the most valuable ones for the company.

The door opens and a woman named Morgan introduces herself. "Oh, do you need any help?"

She is in four-inch heels and wears a short dress. I have everything in my hands, but there is no way this woman was going to lean into my hatchback and grab plastic bins even if I needed help.

"I got it," I say, turning to get the rest of my items. A moment later, Morgan has an arm around me.

"Oh come in, come in, let me get you a drink," she says, leading me into her home. There are four other women here already, wine glasses in hand, grazing over a platter of cheese and crackers set out on the kitchen island. They're all in tailored clothing, with shiny hair, and are speaking in hushed tones about something. Patrick, I'd guess.

The home is gorgeous. There's a large wall of windows overlooking the water, the ceilings are enormous, and the kitchen looks like it was pulled from the pages of an *Architectural Digest*.

"Darlings, this is Gray," Morgan coos, gathering the women alongside her. "Everyone be nice. Gray was Patrick's new assistant."

"Well, not techni—" I start to say, but Morgan talks over me.

"She was the one who called the police, who found him . . ." Morgan presses her fingers to the bridge of her nose. "Who found him dead."

"Oh, love."

"You poor thing."

"It's all so dreadful."

Their words may be meant to soothe me, but they irritate me. As I take them in, I see they're all wearing black and I have the sickening feeling this is some sort of mourning. But also a social event. The way they've blended the two, so shortly after Patrick's death, is unsettling. I should never have agreed to come.

I look over at the sunken living room where I placed my bins and bags, ready to get to work. "It's been a complicated time. Thankfully the Tacoma Police Department are working hard at finding the person who did this to Patrick," I say, sounding like I'm offering some sort of public relations statement.

"Of course they are," Morgan says, handing me a glass of champagne. "Shall we toast to Patrick? A great man and dear friend."

I lift the glass as they all clink theirs against mine, as all eyes are on me. My mouth feels dry. I see Patrick, dead on his carpet, blood pooling around his head. A murderer on the loose. *Jeremiah?*

This is all too soon.

"To Patrick," they repeat, finishing their drinks.

"Now, about our purchases?" One of them says, walking to the living room.

"Right," I say, setting down the still full champagne flute. "So, I brought your orders, along with the new catalogues. I know you all use the online portal, but if you'd like to order with me, you can do that in person tonight." I walk toward the bins and begin opening them up. I have been doing the vast majority of Patrick's deliveries for him the past few months, but this group of women were his most elite clientele. I was able to stop at his condo and get their orders before coming here. While his place is a crime scene, an officer made the exception for me to gather my pre-packaged inventory.

"Any idea of how he died?" one of the women asks as I begin sorting the bags, as if it isn't an incredibly intrusive question. There are six bags included with this drop-off, but I only count five women here.

"It was a murder," I say softly, wondering who these women are? "It was in the *Tacoma Tribune*."

"We saw that," she says. "But we mean, like, who killed him?"

"If I knew that, the case would be solved," I say, setting the bags on the coffee table, and then taking a stack of catalogues from one of the canvas bags.

"Was it awful?" another woman asks. "I've never seen a dead person."

My jaw falls open, shocked at the sensationalism of this conversation. It's all so insensitive. Thank goodness Anna didn't come.

"Look, here are your orders," I say bluntly, not wanting to be here any longer than necessary. "If you want to go through the catalogue, call me about any products you have questions on."

"You need a drink, darling," Morgan says. When I tell her no thanks, she clucks her tongue. "Patrick was right about you. You are a little stiff, aren't you?"

I wonder if Patrick really spoke to these women about me. I can't imagine it. "Well, nonetheless, here are your bags. Looks like Tristan didn't make it. Should I bring it to her home, or—"

Morgan takes the bag from my hand. "I'll get her the goodies. I see her every day at the club."

"Great," I say. "Then I'm just gonna head out."

"You just got here," Morgan says, frowning.

"I have two daughters who need me," I say, making an excuse to leave. "But I'm glad I was able to make this drop-off." I smile tightly, pressing my lips together. They don't even stop me as I leave, taking my now empty plastic bins and finding my own way to the front door. Wondering why these women are so flippant, wondering how in the world they can be reaching for the bags and digging through their products. Oohing and ahhing over face peels and elixirs and tinctures when Patrick is dead.

* * *

Later, I get a text from Anna.

> Anna: *What happened at Morgan's? They want a new rep.*
>
> Me: *No idea. I did the delivery.*
>
> Anna: *She said you were rude. They were offended.*
>
> Me: *They were acting really . . . off. Not realizing the gravity of what has happened.*
>
> Anna: *We're selling a product to make people's lives better, not to bring them down.*
>
> Me: *I think it's all too soon, Anna.*
>
> Anna: *For who? This is my livelihood. There are people in Patrick's circle who count on this income. It can't stop because he is gone.*

I power my phone off, not wanting to read anything else from Anna tonight. She's one of my closest friends and Patrick's sister . . . so why is she acting so callous, so cold? And why is she pretending everything is okay when nothing is?

CHAPTER 11

The next morning after the girls get off to school, I head to the grocery store. I have the day off from the library and I'm using the first few hours of it to catch up on errands. After the week's food is purchased, I stop at the day-old bread store for bagels and baguettes, then make a quick dash into the thrift store to see if there are any waterproof boots in Ruthie's size. I score a lavender pair and even manage to find a marigold sweater that I know Olive will love.

Once home I turn on the radio to a local station of oldies, and begin unloading my groceries. The cold winter day has me hungry, and so I pull out some frozen lentil soup from the freezer, grateful I doubled the batch when I made it last week. While it warms, I eye the French bread, suddenly craving something sweet.

As the soup simmers, I dice the loaf of bread and grab eggs, sugar, and vanilla. I grease a glass baking pan and begin putting together salted caramel bread pudding, my comfiest of comfort foods. After I pop it into the preheated oven, I grab a ladle for the soup just as the doorbell rings.

Twisting my lips, I look at the clock. It's only twelve-thirty, and the girls won't be home for several hours, not that they would ring the bell anyways. I'm not expecting anyone, especially not Anna after our phone call this morning. She was annoyed I turned off my phone last night, and doubly annoyed that I ruined things with Morgan down at the marina. But honestly, I still feel irritated about going to the party at all. Without knowing who did this to Patrick, it felt wrong to move on.

When I look through the peephole I see Boone standing there, running a hand through his hair. I feel a strange sense of relief at seeing him and pull open the door. "I wasn't expecting you."

He shrugs. "I had a few questions for you. Thought this might be easier than having you come into the station."

Holding open the door, I tell him to come in. "It's freezing out there."

"Literally. My driveway was ice this morning."

"So you live in Tacoma?" I ask as he scrapes his boots against the mat outside the house.

He follows me to the kitchen. "I'm in Buckley, got a cabin out there."

"I've never heard of it." Looking over at the stove, I add, "I'm dishing up soup. Are you hungry?"

His eyes widen. "Starved, actually. And yeah, Buckley's about thirty minutes away, still in Pierce County though."

Nodding as I dish up two bowls of soup and carry them to the table, I say, "I can picture you in a cabin, actually."

"Yeah? I built it ten years ago. Supposed to be a getaway. But now, I'm there full-time."

"Has electricity though?"

He chuckles. "Yeah, but no air conditioning. My ex hated that."

"I hope you like lentil soup," I tell him, handing him a napkin and spoon.

"Anything that isn't from a drive-thru is better than I'm used to."

"Oh yeah? No homecooked meals in your cozy cabin?" I sit across from him at the kitchen table. Boone is acting more friendly than he did the last time he was here and I'm grateful. I don't have the energy for a confrontation at the moment.

Dipping his spoon in the soup, he shakes his head. "If you saw the place, you wouldn't call it cozy. Rustic, maybe. Nothing like this place you've got here."

"I'm renting this house, and it's old, but it has character. I like that. I wish it were mine."

"What would you do if it were?"

I smile. "Honestly? I'd take a sledgehammer and knock down the wall over there," I say, pointing, "and make the first floor a great room. One of my neighbors renovated her home like that and it's really welcoming."

"I can see that," he says. "Would be good for your home parties too. That's your thing, right?"

"Something like that," I say, taking a bite of the soup.

"This is really good," Boone says. "Beats the canned chili I buy."

I think of his earlier comment about his ex, and wonder about his life. I remember the police officer at Patrick's condo, joking about Boone having a mid-life crisis.

"So you mentioned some questions?" As comfortable as this conversation seems to be, I also don't have any interest in getting too chatty with an officer of the law. This man is a detective and I don't want him digging into my life. I have too many secrets for that.

"I was wondering about what you did for Patrick, mostly. Trying to understand this business."

I frown. "Didn't Elle tell you about her company?"

"A bit, but I don't quite understand what you did for Patrick."

"I did deliveries for him. My garage is filled with inventory."

"But I heard that last night you were at his condo, getting some of the product."

"I was, because there was a party for his VIP clients. He handled those orders. I don't think he trusted me enough to deal with his higher end buyers."

Boone scrapes the bottom of his bowl, and I can tell the wheels in his mind are turning. "So he didn't trust you implicitly?"

I set down my spoon and lay my elbows on the table. "I don't know how much Patrick trusted me. We hadn't known one another long."

"Long enough for him to foot your daughter's ballet lessons though?"

"How do you know about that?"

Boone leans back in his chair. "It's my job to know, Gray."

Feeling flustered, I'm relieved when the timer for the oven goes off. I jump from my chair and grab a pot holder. I pull out the bread pudding and the kitchen fills with the sweet aroma of sugar and bread.

"You trying to make me lose my train of thought?" he asks, chuckling.

"It wasn't the plan, but it's working I think." I set the pan on a trivet on the counter, then close the oven, turning it off. "Look, Patrick and I got along. I think he saw it as a mentorship. And he needed some help with his business, and he knew I needed some extra money. It wasn't more than that."

I turn to the coffee maker, and begin making a pot as Boone's rough voice grounds me in reality. "My job is to find Patrick's killer, so we're on the same team here, unless you're not telling me something?"

"I'm telling you everything." *Mostly.*

"Good. Then tell me what you know about Karen Shepard."

I frown, reaching for two coffee mugs. "I don't know a Karen Shepard. Should I?"

"She used to be under Patrick, or he signed her up — you know how the pyramid works better than me."

"It's not a pyramid," I say, irritated. "And I don't know her. But as you know, I've only been working with Patrick for a handful of months. You should ask Anna. She knows way more than me about Patrick's business and his downline."

Boone stands, joining me next to the coffee pot. "So tell me, if I wanted to sign up to sell these vitamins, what would I do?"

I bite my bottom lip. "Well, I'd have you fill out some paperwork online, and then you'd be directly under me, so when you sold products, I'd get a small commission."

"And the person above you, Patrick, what would he get?"

"A portion of the commission as well."

Boone give a tight laugh. "Right, like a pyramid?"

"If you read the Federal Trade Commission's website, you'd know multi-level marketing isn't a Ponzi scheme. It's legitimate products being sold for fair prices, with no one losing."

His lips twitch, and he reaches for the coffee pot, pouring us mugs. "You did your research?"

I roll my eyes. "You think I'd just join some random business without reading about it?"

"I don't know." He takes a drink of the coffee. "I honestly don't know much about you at all. You seem to have arrived in Tacoma a year ago as if out of thin air."

My jaw tenses at that, wanting to change the subject. "Do you want bread pudding? It's delicious."

"Please." He watches me as I dish us both up portions, then carry them to the kitchen table. He sets my coffee in front of me, and I try not to reveal just how uncomfortable I am about treading that close to why I am in Tacoma.

"Why are you really here? You could have gotten all of this from Elle or Anna."

"To be frank, they aren't being very cooperative."

I swallow. "Am I a suspect again?"

Boone's eyes level with mine. "If you were, I'd have already read you your rights."

The kitchen fills with tension for a moment too long. Boone's eyes lock with mine, not letting me go, and for a fraction of a minute I have the strangest feeling. Like I don't want him to look away.

Finally though, I sit down, and he does the same, and we drink our coffee in silence. My mind reeling with the information that I am absolutely not a suspect, which means Jeremiah isn't either. So what is Boone's visit about?

He looks down at is food, shaking his head. "Damn, this is incredible."

A soft smile spreads across my face. "Thanks," I finally say. "I want to help you. But I don't know Karen. Anna is honestly the best person to talk to about all of this. I'm a small fish in this company. Maybe I'm not even a fish. Maybe I'm just bait."

"If you're the bait, someone is using you. Do you feel used?"

I take a bite of my bread pudding. "Not at all. I feel like I have a purpose, like I'm finally living the life I want."

Boone nods slowly, chewing his food. "I'm a little jealous of that."

"Really? But you have the prestigious job, the cabin of your own."

"It's all relative I suppose, huh?"

I nod, knowing it's true. My sister wives back at Garden Temple feel their lives are purposeful, and yet for me, it wasn't. Not even close.

"So what is the life you really want?" I ask Boone, knowing it's much too intimate for a detective here for business. But everything about this encounter feels personal.

He looks around the kitchen. "Honestly? I feel like I need a sledgehammer to deal with what's left of it. Knock it all to the ground."

"Sounds ominous."

"I lost a child," he tells me, running a hand over his jaw. "It changed everything. Changed me."

My breath catches. I lost a child too. A daughter, only two days old. A year after Abel was born, two years before Olive. After that loss, I was never the same.

And I see now, that on every level, Boone is more than meets the eye. Which means he is more like Jeremiah than I thought.

And the last thing I need is him getting too close. Close enough to learn my secrets, unbury my past.

Because Boone isn't the only one who has lost a child. I have too.

CHAPTER 12

Boone's confession rattles me. But I have to say something.

The room is so quiet you could hear a pin drop.

"I'm sorry for your loss," I finally manage.

My words are spoken at the same moment he pushes back from the table. "I should go," Boone says.

I stand too then, feeling like too much has been said, shared. Confidences made where there shouldn't be any. I have never had a conversation like this with a man before. Candid, real. Vulnerable. Garden Temple may have preached honesty, but no man there was transparent. Boone, though, with his tired eyes and rumpled clothes, has sat at my table, being open with me in a way I don't recognize. He is more real than any man I've ever known; realer even than Patrick.

"Thanks for lunch, Gray." He turns to me, by the front door. "And thanks for the talk."

"It was just for work, right?" My voice is too high, my words still falling flat.

"Right," he says with a smirk. "Work."

I watch him get in his beat-up red Jeep Cherokee, and watch him drive away. Looking up and down the street after he's gone. Looking for something, someone. Looking for a ghost that isn't there. Looking for Jeremiah.

* * *

I spend the rest of the afternoon organizing orders and inventory in the garage. It's easy work, but it forces me to keep thinking about Patrick. His murderer is on the loose, and while I appreciate Boone being assigned to the case, he isn't exactly coming up with a suspect list.

Why was he asking questions about the ins and outs of how wELLEness is structured? It makes me wonder if there is foul play within the company. The idea turns my stomach to knots. Maybe Elle isn't what I thought.

But could she be so villainous as to kill Patrick? It doesn't seem remotely plausible.

I spend the evening helping the girls with homework and listening to Olive explain her new science lessons. It is the first time in her life she has studied anything scientific and she finds it fascinating. It is moments like this — when she is explaining how scientists test out different theories until they have evidence — that remind me why we're here. Not at Garden Temple. I am more than happy for my girls to have faith in the unknown, but I want them to understand the way the world works. The way matter moves, the way humans evolve.

The next day I'm running late — I stayed up late reading online articles about multi-level marketing and scams. I ended up finding a podcast called *The Dream*, and listened to it for hours. It's confusing. On one hand I believe in the products wELLEness provides, and the way it gets into the hands of consumers — but is it all a gimmick? Is it really that impossible for distributors to make back their initial investment? I know the wELLEness starter pack costs twenty-six hundred dollars. Patrick offered me the job assisting him to pay down the outlay. But how are other people affording that? It's one thing to come to a home party and spend thirty bucks on some face peels, but is that really the consumer wELLEness is after? I want to know. Need to know.

I spent way too many years in a cult to just get caught up in another trap.

The girls are happy to eat leftover bread pudding for breakfast and while they eat, I text Anna.

Me: *Thinking of you. Need anything?*

Anna: *OMG you're an angel. Can you bring me a box of the new catalogues? I remember you got a box last month?*

I frown. Why is she so hung up on the business when her brother is dead? Not that I'm any better, considering my Google search history last night. And we all cope in different ways. Maybe her way is pouring herself into her work.

Me: *Sure. I'll be there in 30*

On the way to the bus stop, I remind the girls that they are both signed up for the after-school science club. Olive groans, saying she's too old for that, but Ruthie is excited. She's the one who brought home the flier a few weeks ago begging me to sign them up. Since it is sponsored by local engineers and free of charge for students, I made a point to register them both. "It's once a week for a few months. The bus will bring you home right at dinnertime," I tell Olive. "Who knows, you might even make some new friends."

After the girls get on the bus, I grab the box of catalogues from the garage and put them in my backseat. The drive to Anna's is quick and a few minutes later I'm parked in front of her home. It's a large house in the heart of the city. A fully remodeled craftsman home that has me wondering what my life would have been like if my parents had never died. If I hadn't ended up with my aunt and uncle, with Jeremiah.

Anna didn't take a sledgehammer to any of this. Her husband Jasper is a lawyer and was the one who handled the financing of this upgrade. I know all of this because Anna is very keen on discussing these sorts of details. It's in direct juxtaposition with her carefully curated image of urban farmer with chickens and kombucha-making farmers' market shopper. She may like the idea of being an organic free-loving woman, but she also loves having a housekeeper and gardener. I also know her husband desperately wants a child and Anna refuses. It's a big rift in their marriage. But I'm not one to judge other peoples relationships. It's not like my track record is to be envied.

And as much as I appreciate Anna's generosity with me, I also know she is one of those people who likes people to think of them in a certain way.

I'm familiar with these sorts of women. I had one as a sister wife. Lydia was so caught up in appearing holier and more devout than anyone else in the family. It seemed exhausting, always trying to put on a shell for the world. But I didn't judge Lydia and I'm not judging Anna either. We all have our own reasons for the things we do, and I'm not one to point fingers. I'm not exactly honest about much myself.

I knock on her front door and she opens it with a smile on her face. "Oh, Gray. You're such a godsend." She takes the box from me and I follow her inside. "It's been a whirlwind here the last few days."

My first thought is Patrick, the whirlwind surrounding the death of her brother. Reporters, far-flung family, everyone who would want to hear from her on her grave loss.

But she's not thinking of him. Of that. No, her home is filled with everything wELLEness. Huge stacks of product on the large kitchen table. Her office that's right off the kitchen has a few people I vaguely recognize inside, hovering over a laptop.

"What's going on?" I ask, confused.

A young woman with a short black bob comes in the front door behind me, with a tray of to-go coffees in her hand. She begins handing them out. "Your double oat milk latte." She passes the white to-go cup to Anna, who takes it graciously.

"That's Marley," Anna says as the woman walks toward the office. "She's my new assistant."

"Since when?" I ask, remembering the conversation only a few months ago between her and Patrick and me. She was irritated that her brother was able to take on an employee, feeling frustrated that her husband wasn't open to it. He didn't think she was pulling in enough of an income from wELLEness to justify the hired help. Patrick, on the other hand, had been moving up in the company, quickly.

"Since yesterday." Her lips twitch. "Come here," she says, dragging me outside to the back patio where her free-range chickens peck for seed. "So, I have pretty big news."

My eyes widen. "Is there news on Patrick?"

Anna scrunches up her face. "No, actually there is nothing new. That I've heard."

"Okay," I say slowly. "Boone, the detective, was over yesterday and had all these questions. About wELLEness, and Patrick and—"

"What about wELLEness?" Anna cuts in.

"How the business model works, mostly."

"Oh, okay, I just hate the idea of him prying into our lives. When you say he was over, over where?"

"My house," I say, shrugging. "We had soup."

Anna's eyes lift. "Soup?"

I nod. "But that doesn't matter. What is your news?"

"I took over wELLEness."

"What happened to Elle?"

Anna shrugs. "She wanted out, everything with Patrick really struck a nerve. And I wanted in. I know Jasper didn't originally see the potential earning power of this company, but I have a lot of ideas, a lot of ambition. And this is the opportunity of a lifetime."

Chills run over me, head to toe. "Patrick's murderer is on the loose, Anna. Isn't this a little . . . soon?"

She crosses her arms, irritated. "Patrick would want me to be happy."

"Of course he would," I say. "But Anna, what if there is foul play at work here? With this company?"

"Foul play? God, Gray. I love you like a sister but sometimes I wonder what is going through your mind. This was an accident. A tragic accident, but no one is trying to destroy anything."

"He's your brother, Anna. Don't you care about who did this? How can you worry yourself with wELLEness when you haven't even buried him?"

Anna presses her lips into a tight line. "Yes, Patrick is my brother, but it's more complicated than that. You wouldn't understand, you don't have family. But Patrick and I have been through a lot together."

"And doesn't that long history mean you at least owe him a few weeks to get his affairs in order?"

Anna scoffs. "You're judging me. And that hurts, Gray. I'm a woman trying to support other women in business. And after all I've done for you, I thought you'd be happy for me."

I have a hard time looking her in the eye, her judgement feels all off and I'm not sure how to say that without offending her. Boone had said she wasn't being cooperative. And coupled with her new ownership of the company, it makes me wonder just who Anna is. Because this doesn't seem like the person I met last fall in the library, who pulled me in, under her wing.

The back door opens and Marley pokes in her head. "Hey, hate to interrupt, but there's a call for you, Anna. It seems important."

"Of course," Anna says. "One sec." Then she turns to me. "I know there are loose ends with Patrick, and that is tragic, but we have keep moving forward, Gray. Let the police do their job and we have to do ours."

I follow her inside, at a loss for words. She mistakes it for understanding and wraps me into a hug. "Thank you for stopping by. I was excited to tell you my news face to face. And I know the party at the marina was a bust, but maybe with a little encouragement you can get back out there and put on a brave face?"

"Sure," I say, breathless as we walk to the door. "I've got to get to work. We'll take later."

"Of course we will. You were my friend first, remember. Your loyalty lies with me." She is laughing as she says this but the smile on my face is completely false.

If my loyalty lies anywhere, it's with myself.

I haven't come this far in my life to pledge allegiance to another mad man.

When I met Anna, I thought she was my saving grace. But being close to her right now feels like a death sentence. And I sure don't want to wind up in hell.

CHAPTER 13

As I drive away from Anna's my stomach is twisted in knots. Her acquiring the business makes no sense . . . and I wish I was closer with Elle to call her and ask, but we've never even had a conversation one-on-one. It feels like too big of a leap.

I roll down the window even though it is freezing out, but I need the fresh air. My mind is all jumbled and I want it clear. Anna was acting so odd on so many counts — the new employees materializing out of thin air, the lack of emotion over losing her brother.

Then I think of Olive and Ruthie. They lost Abel, their brother, only a year ago. But it wasn't like this. It wasn't murder, wasn't final. There is hope, with Abel, somehow. That one day things will be different and he will be in our lives again.

I wish it were now. Wish he were here, in our day-to-day lives, and not just nested deep in our hearts. I miss him, and can't imagine losing him to the hands of a killer.

But maybe a mother's love is different than the love a sibling has? I never had a brother or sister, but I did lose my mom and dad.

And even now, as I look back at my memories, I didn't sob uncontrollably for weeks after they died in the horrific car crash. I moved to Garden Temple and was forced into a new identity. I lied my tears away and trusted my aunt when she told me they were in a better place.

Anna isn't a religious person though, she isn't setting her grief aside and letting God handle it. She is acting like Patrick isn't dead, or worse, that he is but she's choosing not to grieve this loss.

I turn into the employee parking lot and grab my tote bag with my packed lunch. I walk briskly into the building, wanting to get away from the cold. Inside the library, I smile and wave to my coworkers, looking over my work for the day. There are several carts of books ready for shelving, and once I've placed a lanyard around my neck indicating I work here, I roll the cart to the library floor.

My cart is filled with children's books and for that I am grateful. It's not that I mind the aisles of the nonfiction titles or the mysteries, but at this time of day, the children's section is like comfort food, filled with tired mothers trying to entertain their toddlers with picture books and puzzles. It's nostalgic. Diaper bags and bottles bringing me to the past — which I realize might be considered a strange sentiment. I'm not that old, I could have a baby myself — I'm not even thirty — but it feels like a lifetime ago when I carried Ruthie on my hip. A lifetime I loved so tenderly. Having little ones was never a burden — it was something I cherished with every fiber of my being. Jeremiah made it so that I didn't want more, not with him. But mothering little ones was my favorite season of life.

So, seeing the toddlers here in the library, giggling and throwing blocks and being read to in a rocking chair, makes me reminiscent of a season of life that was cut too short. But the sounds filtering around me as I put *Angelina Ballerina* in place, and well-worn copies of *Winnie the Pooh* back on the shelf, help pass time and let my mind rest on topics less burdensome than Patrick's murder.

After I finish in the children's section I head for another cart, this time loaded down with travel books. Each spine sending me to a different destination. Tahiti. Ireland. Quebec. Each distant land offering the distance I crave for the girls and me. It's a fantasy, to disappear on an airplane and never return.

Reality is much more somber. When I pick up a book to shelve titled *Family Vacation Made Easy*, my stomach twists.

Family is so complicated — and a vacation with all of my children seems impossible. And it's not just the financial restraints. My family isn't whole — Abel is with his father, and I haven't seen him once since we left.

I run my hand over the cover of the book, a grinning family of four at the beach, rushing into the waves. I think the last time I saw one of my children in the water was at Ruthie's baptism.

It had been such an awful day. And it was supposed to be happy, but I was the one who ruined it for everyone.

We had all gone out to Moses Lake for the day; it was a big deal for the congregation to leave the compound. But it was August and so hot, and everyone was tired of the heat. Having a Sunday church service and potluck was something to lift everyone's morale, and there were four kids getting baptized, which added to the excitement.

Ruthie had been so excited. She'd taken the confirmation class in Sunday school, had recited the verses that she'd been asked to memorize. She donned a pure white dress that I had sewn myself and joined her father in the large lake.

He'd dunked her head beneath the water and when she emerged it was with the promise of a new life, reborn, dedicated to the Lord.

It felt like she'd been plunged into a promise that she wasn't old enough to make. I remember tears in my eyes as she ran toward me, arms spread wide, smile on her face. "I did it," she'd said, beaming up at me.

"You sure did," I said, kissing her head.

She grinned. "Next big thing is getting married."

I swallowed, heart stopping, hating the words on her lips. Many little girls dream of getting married one day, but the knowledge of what Jeremiah wanted for Olive was too real for me to play it cool.

"You won't be getting married for a long, long time," I had told her, my voice harsh enough for her to flinch.

Abel and Olive were with us, and Abel spoke. "Maybe not, but Olive will be married soon, and so will I."

"You're barely fifteen," I'd said tightly. "And Olive is still a child."

"It's her duty," Abel had said, indignant. "She needs to provide a child for the glory of God. It's her highest calling."

"Stop it," I'd said as Jeremiah joined us.

"Stop what?" He'd asked me, looking at his children. At least some of them, his other wives had children with him too.

"Mother is once again forgetting the role of women in our fold," Abel had said with his shoulders back, looking at his father with reverence.

"Is this about Olive getting married?" Jeremiah looked at me with a stern eye. "Enough with this, Grace. Enough. Especially today."

I pressed my lips in a fine line, looking at my daughters, my son, feeling like no one was on my side. Hating that there had to be sides at all. But there did, and there were, and I was alone.

I knew then that we would go.

And that Abel wouldn't join us when I took the girls and left. They were young enough to save, but he was bigger than me — taller and stronger — and I didn't want to fight him physically. The emotional fight I knew I was in for with Olive and Ruthie would be big enough to tackle. They believed Garden Temple was destined for greatness, God's land, and God's people. I knew that when I took them from their home they would hate me.

Now, as I shelf *Family Vacation Made Easy*, I wish there was a manual on Family Separation Made Easy because I would devour that one. Because even though I chose to leave my son, I miss Abel, and so do the girls.

So, so much.

Which brings me back to Anna and Patrick.

How could a sister forget a brother so fast? It doesn't add up.

Because Abel has been gone a year and not a day goes by that the three of us don't talk about him. And he isn't even dead.

Something doesn't add up. And I need to figure out what it is. I can't fix things with Abel right now, but I might be able to help find out the truth about my friend.

CHAPTER 14

My shift ends, I zip up my winter coat and grab my empty lunch box. My eyes are heavy and I wish there was a break room with a coffee pot where I could grab a quick caffeine fix before heading out for the rest of my day. I quickly tell my coworkers goodbye before walking to my car. For a wintery afternoon, the sky is blue and I'm glad for a few more hours of daylight.

As I drive through Tacoma, I decide to pull into a café Patrick and I went to a few times together. I park my car and enter the coffee shop. With Valentine's Day right around the corner, there are pink and red paper hearts hanging from the ceiling, and holiday-themed drinks on the menu.

"May I please have a Lavender Love Latte?" I ask the barista.

"What's your name?"

"Grace," I say, then realizing my mistake, I add, "Gray. My name is Gray."

Someone touches my shoulder from behind. "Gray?"

I turn, seeing Boone. My throat goes dry. Did he just hear me tell the barista my name is Grace? And what is he doing here anyway? Following me?

He doesn't say anything about it, instead he points to the menu board. "What's with these frouffy drinks? There isn't even drip coffee on the menu."

The barista smiles widely, interjecting. "I can make you an Americano. Basically the same thing."

Boone clears his throat, offers a shoulder shrug. "Nah, I'll just have what she's having."

After he pays he joins me at the end of the bar where I'm waiting for my drink. He looks tired, probably the same as me.

"What are you doing in this part of town?" I ask him, remembering how yesterday he told me he lived a fair distance from here. The police station is on the other side of town.

"In the neighborhood. I just officially closed up the crime scene over at Patrick's place."

Nodding, I ask, "Any suspects?"

Boone runs a hand over his jaw, eyes fixed on mine. "Not at liberty to tell, Grace."

So he did hear me. I choose not to engage in a conversation about that because it won't take me anywhere good. Thankfully the cheery barista calls out our names before there is too long of an awkward silence.

We take our coffees from the bar and walk to the exit. On the sidewalk Boone and I stand looking at one another. I'm unsure of what to say — in my kitchen it felt like he was a friend, or at least someone I could trust. But now it feels like there is a divide between us. What happened in the last twenty-four hours?

Boone takes a drink from his paper cup. His face curls up in disgust. "What the hell is this?"

I bite back a smile. "A Lavender Love Latte."

"It tastes like soap." He walks over to the trash and tosses his cup in.

I take a sip. "I think it's delicious."

He shakes his head. "You seem smart enough, but we're gonna have to agree to disagree on that one."

"It was nice seeing you," I say. "And I hope you're getting somewhere with Patrick. He was a good man, and he deserves to rest in peace, with his killer found."

Boone nods slowly. "Everyone does, good or bad. Eternity is a long ass time."

A chill runs down my spine, and I'm not sure I agree with him. The man I killed deserved it and then some. The idea of him peacefully enjoying eternity makes me sick.

I give Boone a small smile. "Any case, I'm glad you're on the job."

Boone's eyes fix on mine for a beat too long before he lifts a hand, giving me a two-finger wave. He then points to the café. "I still need a cup of coffee. I'm gonna go order that Americano now. Wish me luck?"

"Good luck," I say, as he pulls open the door and enters the shop, leaving me on the sidewalk. I hardly know the man but I liked standing out here with him; it felt like he would be able to keep me safe.

Even as I think it, I hate myself for it. When I left Garden Temple I promised myself that I would never again rely on a man for protection. It was time I learned to protect myself.

Still, standing here alone on the sidewalk leaves me wanting something more. I sip my drink, looking down the street, toward the waterfront. Since it's just after three and knowing the girls won't be home for two hours, thanks to the science club, I start walking in the direction of Patrick's place. All day my gut has been telling me that something is off with Anna and knowing that the crime scene is cleared out makes the breaking and entering I'm considering seem less insane.

After a ten-minute walk, I'm out front of his condo. His Tesla is still in his parking spot. How long will it be there? Do he and Anna have any other family? I don't even know.

Boone was right, the police tape is gone and there is nothing indicating that Patrick's condo is any different from the other ones in his complex. I walk around back, like I did only a few days ago, but instead of seeing a smashed sliding glass door, I see it's been reframed with new glass.

I hadn't considered how I'd get inside, but as I step closer to the glass door, I notice the window in the dining room doesn't have a screen. I walk through the landscape rockery and press my palm to the low window. It moves. Exhaling with relief, I look around. With no one in sight, I push the unlocked window open the rest of the way and climb up, tossing my purse on the ground as I awkwardly jump onto the sill. I manage to get inside, thinking that Olive would probably have a good one-liner to toss at me about my entrance. I'm glad she isn't here — glad no one else is here. I want to look at Patrick's place without any prying eyes. I might find something that the officers wouldn't have considered evidence.

Grabbing my purse and crossing it over my body, my walk through his place is eerie — it's cold and dark, nothing like the vibrant man who lived here. I run my fingertips over the kitchen counter, see that his fridge is empty, his garbage can too. And I wonder if Anna took care of that. If she was able to clean up his life before she set it aside?

I walk into his bedroom. I've never been in here before. The bed is low to the ground and modern, made perfectly. I pull open a dresser drawer, seeing folded shirts, socks tucked into one another. His closet is full of pressed suits, a hanger full of ties. And I wonder what happens to all these pieces of his life now that he is gone. A yard sale? A charity shop? Grief catches in my throat. I hate not knowing who did this to him and why.

Leaving his bedroom, I walk to the office. The day I found Patrick dead I had pulled open his desk drawer, looking for a clue, but had been stopped short when the officers arrived on the scene. Now though, no one is here, and I can look freely.

Most of the drawers are empty, but there are a few with old paperwork from wELLEness. Invoices, shipment slips, a file labeled TAXES — inside are dozens of receipts from business lunches and coffee dates. I can see why the police didn't want to pull these items into evidence, they are irrelevant business paperwork. But as I'm about to dismiss the piles of paper I'm shuffling through, my eye catches on something more official.

> *IN THE JUSTICE COURT OF TACOMA, PIERCE COUNTY, STATE OF WASHINGTON*
>
> *Patrick T. Kelly, Applicant*
> *vs.*
> *Karen Shepard, Adverse party*
>
> *TEMPORARY ORDER OF PROTECTION AGAINST STALKING, AGGRAVATED STALKING, OR HARRASSMENT*

It's dated from last summer before I even met Patrick. The only thing that catches in my mind is the name. Karen. Didn't Boone ask me about someone named Karen yesterday? I think he said Shepard. My first thought is she is a suspect. And if so, I want to know why. She clearly was doing something that was causing problems for Patrick. Were they romantically involved? I think not, considering this was buried in the receipts folder for wELLEness. What was their connection then?

A car alarm goes off in the parking lot and I jump, scared from the sound. My heart pounds as I consider getting caught in this apartment. I consider my girls. This is not a risk I should be taking. The last thing I need is to get in trouble with the law. I fold the paper in half, sliding it into my purse. The I move quickly through the apartment, leaving the same way I came.

CHAPTER 15

At night, after the girls get in bed, I do some digging. In my bedroom, with my smartphone in hand, I type "Karen Shepard, Tacoma WA" into the search bar.

Her name immediately pops up directing me to a Facebook account. Since I don't have any social media, I can't see much on Facebook, but can see enough to know she lives in Tacoma and she even lists her phone number. I screenshot it before looking deeper.

In her job history, she lists that she currently works at a local grocery store, but before that, she was a wELLEness consultant.

Okay, so that's how she knew Patrick.

Going back to her profile, I look at her photo. She looks a little older than me, maybe, with blonde hair and light eyes. I can see some highlight posts that she shares with everyone. They are short posts, made sporadically over the last year, about her son Sonny.

- *Things are looking up!!! Home & healthy — two words that mean the world to us!*
- *He's a fighter! Another round of chemo today. Love you Sonny-Shine!*

- *The cancer is back. Praying for light at the end of this tunnel.*
- *My little boy turned nine at St. Mark's. Best hospital staff in the world!!*
- *Sonny has a post-surgery infection. Headed back to be admitted.*
- *Thank you for the love and support. I'm still stunned that my baby has cancer. Doesn't seem fair. My heart is broken.*
- *Finally got a diagnosis. Sonny has stage three brain cancer. Please pray.*

Karen's words send a wave of emotion through me. Her family has been through so much in such a short amount of time.

As tempted as I am to call her and ask about Patrick, after reading this, it doesn't feel appropriate. I'm about to forget the restraining order all together when I see another post. This one cryptic enough to have me wondering if maybe I am headed in the right direction.

- I can't legally say anything negative about the company I used to work for but I am so over being bullied!!!!! GROW UP!!!!

Her latest post made it seem like her son was on the mend, so maybe a text from me won't be entirely out of line. A text is less invasive than a phone call, right? Deciding I have nothing to lose, I type out a text and send it to the number she has listed.

> Me: *Hi, my name is Gray and I used to work for Patrick Kelly. I know you did business with him too. Not sure if you heard but he died a few days ago.*

But instead of a reply, it immediately bounces back, saying the number is out of service. Considering it's Facebook, this number could have been listed here a decade ago. I click my phone off, and lie back against my pillows, trying to make sense of the day. Of Anna's intensity and lack of empathy surrounding Patrick. Running into Boone and feeling oddly safe in his presence. Breaking into a condo — risking everything for what? An error message.

No, that risk needs a bigger reward.

Tomorrow after the girls leave for school, I'm going to that grocery store and I am going to have a talk with Karen Shepard.

* * *

When I arrive at Save N Clip, there is no guarantee that Karen will be working. Not wanting to draw attention to myself, I grab a cart and begin shopping for the food I need for the week anyways. The store is a ghost town, and maybe it is the early morning hours, or maybe it's because it isn't exactly a quality food mart.

I've never been to this grocery store before but am personally pleasantly surprised with it. I can't afford the fancy co-ops in town or the organic grocery stores where it's $75 for a single bag of food. Save N Clip is a grocery outlet, mostly discontinued products and day-old produce. But I don't mind bruised apples or nearly expired cans of garbanzo beans. Growing up with limited resources at Garden Temple meant being thankful for what we did have.

And right now I'm thankful for the deeply discounted brand name sugary cereal that will make the girls squeal in delight. I add two boxes to the cart and keep pushing, grabbing a container of Greek yogurt and a bag of Valentine's candies that might be a year old. I figure the preservatives in the hard candy will have left them fresh enough.

As I finish my shopping, I head to a checkout lane, my eyes widening as I see Karen tying an apron on and stepping up to a register. She's just getting to work, so my timing is perfect. Maybe she had to wait until Sonny got off to school, just like I had to wait until the girls caught the bus.

I begin unloading my groceries on the black conveyor belt, choosing my words carefully as I get closer.

"Hi, this might sound odd, but are you Karen Shepard?"

She brightens, her full cheeks sparkly pink from blush and her eyelashes thick and fake. Her hair is curled, and her nails are long and acrylic. She is not the typical wELLEness client, but I am not naive enough to not realize there is often a story underneath the surface.

"Who's asking?" she asks, and I can tell right away she is a people person. I bet she was great at direct sales. It's one of my weaknesses, letting people get close enough to feel comfortable.

"I'm Gray West, and I used to work with Patrick Kelly."

Her smile fades, and she shakes her head. "I'm not supposed to talk about him. Or his shitty business. Excuse my language."

Knowing I need to tread lightly to not ruin my in with her, I say, "It's okay, I know you two had a . . . falling out . . ."

Karen snorts. "Falling out? That man tried to destroy my life when I was at my most vulnerable." She grabs my boxes of cereal, scanning the food as she talks. "I feel awful that he died, was murdered," she adds in a whisper, "but honestly, I'm not surprised."

Her flippancy shocks me. "Really?" I counter. "He was good to me."

"Maybe he changed his ways. But I doubt it. He still in business with his sister?" I nod and Karen shrugs, counting my apples before clicking her nails across the keypad on her register. "Were you in his downline?"

"Just recently. But I was mostly working *for* him, doing his deliveries."

She clucks her tongue. "Why didn't he just have orders shipped to people's houses?"

"He wanted the personal touch."

"Probably another sales tactic he learned from the almighty Elle. Or maybe Treydon, I remember he was all about the *next big thing*. Full of hot air like Pat." She finishes checking me out, then looks around the store, being sure no one else is around. There isn't. This store is nearly empty still. "But I'd be careful if I were you. The cops came to my house, asking about how I knew Patrick. Why he took a restraining order out against me. It seems messy."

"Why *was* there a restraining order?"

Karen cackles, a little too sharp. "I met Patrick at a hotel for one of his intro seminars. Totally bought his BS when I was at my lowest. Desperate for cash to pay for my son's medical bills. He talked a big talk. I bought in, only to learn what a bunch of garbage I was peddling. Not to mention there's no way someone at the bottom can rise in the ranks. It's a total scam."

Careful not to say too much, I think about Boone's analysis of wELLEness, calling it a pyramid scheme. But is Karen just bitter over what life has thrown her way or was Patrick, this man I trusted, who took me in under his wing — who paid for Ruthie's ballet classes for goodness' sake — using me too?

"I'm sorry for everything you went through. Sounds like you've had a really hard year."

She narrows her eyes. "How did you know where to find me? Who I was?"

I swallow, feeling cornered. I decide honesty is the best policy. "I found the restraining order at Patrick's apartment. I looked you up online and saw your photo, some posts about your son. I wasn't trying to pry, I'm just trying to figure out who killed my friend."

She levels her gaze at me and a chill runs up my spine. She is no longer laughing and sparkly. She's ice cold. "You think I did it?"

Flustered, I shake my head. "No, not at all. I trust the police. I just . . . I'm trying to understand."

"Let me help clear it up for you — your buddy Patrick was a con artist, and you've been duped."

CHAPTER 16

Karen ended our conversation even though I didn't want to leave. She called her manager over, asking him about some new discounts, essentially letting me know there was no more space in her day to talk with me.

I left frustrated, without any concrete answers, and now I can't stop thinking about the incident at the grocery store. It's been a few days and still, I'm conflicted. A big part of me wants to go back and apologize for the whole thing. I wasn't calling Karen a killer, but there are parts of her story that still don't add up. Clearly she knew all the major players at wELLEness, but she didn't explain the restraining order. Though I can read between the lines. She felt conned and desperate, and tried to get Patrick to own up to his part. It could have gone from a genuine concern to a hostile situation quickly. But I saw the venom in Karen's eyes — her shiny veneer wasn't long-lasting.

It's Saturday and the girls and are making Valentine's Day cards for the class party on Wednesday. At Garden Temple we didn't recognize most holidays, and Valentine's Day was one we ignored. But when we left, it was the one I remembered best from my childhood. I wanted to recreate it for my girls.

At stores, they're selling cardboard punch-out cards, but I remember homemade ones with doilies and glitter, pom poms and brightly colored stickers. The girls and I have all our goodies spread out on the kitchen table, and we're enjoying the cupcakes our neighbor Kendall dropped off earlier this morning, saying, "Just made a big batch with the kids and thought we'd share!"

It was a small gesture but it meant a lot, and made me wonder how I could reciprocate.

"Who are you making a card for, Mom?" Ruthie asks.

With scissors in hand, I cut out a heart from a piece of red construction paper. "I think I'll just help you guys. You have a lot to make. There are twenty-two kids in each of your classes."

"I bet Olive is making one for Tomas." Ruthie giggles but Olive does not find it funny.

"Be quiet," she says. "And I am making him one because he is in my class. Mom says we have to do one for everybody."

Choosing my words, I ask as casually as possible, while reaching for a glue stick, "Who's Tomas?"

Ruthie pipes in. "Only the cutest boy in the whole wide world."

"Ruthie!" I laugh, eyebrows raised. "Is that appropriate?" My old way of looking at the world seems to creep in more often than I'd like. Because when I look at her across the table, licking the frosting off a vanilla cupcake, I'm reminded that she's just a little girl having fun.

"He is cute," Olive says with a shrug. "But that's not why I like him."

"Why do you like him?" I ask, appreciating her honesty.

She sprinkles purple glitter over her creation. "Because he is really smart. He's not like other boys in sixth grade. Smart enough to want to be my partner in science club."

I give a closed-lip smile. "I like the sound of that." Changing the topic from boys, I say, "Tell me what you learned in science club. Something about organic farming?"

Ruthie jumps into the conversation again. "Yes, and how all-natural and all-organic mean different things. Like some things that are organic aren't called that cause it's too expensive."

Olive nods. "Yeah but some things that are organic aren't necessarily good for you. It still depends on what the ingredients are. Just using organic shampoo doesn't mean it's good for the environment."

"Well, that's interesting, isn't it?"

"Tomas says that's a bad word."

I laugh. "Interesting?"

Olive nods, pursing her lips together like she has the whole world figured out. Maybe she does. "Yeah, it's like a filler word."

"Okay," I say. "Well then I think the lesson at science club offers a lot of new considerations when buying things."

"I agree," Olive says. "Next week we're doing experiments."

Ruthie's shoulders shake as she laughs. "Won't that be *interesting*?" she asks.

Olive rolls her eyes and continues on with her cutting as Ruthie's laugh turns into a frown. Getting out of her chair, she walks over to the back door. She points out the window. "I think I saw Daddy," she says. "Outside."

"What?" I push away from the table. The sky is overcast and it's been raining on and off all morning. She may have seen a shadow, or a neighbor. "Where?"

"By the tree," she says.

I walk to the back door, pulling it open, and go outside, heart racing. Is Jeremiah here, watching us, waiting? I wrap my arms around myself as I run to the tree, looking around for any signs of people. "Jeremiah?" I shout. "Are you here?" The question doesn't sound as absurd as it should. "Are you?"

There is no answer, but I run around the house anyways, looking back to the window, where the girls are now pressing their noses against the glass, watching me. But no one is here. It is storm clouds and drizzle and an empty street.

I head back inside, telling Ruthie she must have mistaken a shadow for him. Olive smirks. "Or a ghost."

Grabbing the plate of cupcakes, I tell them each to have another; I take one too. I'd rather ruin dinner than ruin our good mood.

* * *

Sunday mornings are always strange, now that we don't head to church for all-day services. Anna invited us over for the Super Bowl and even though I know nothing about football, I'm glad. I want to talk with her and make sure she is actually okay. The more I've thought about it, the more I wonder if her bizarre decision to purchase wELLEness was a response to her grief. Sometimes loss makes us do unfathomable things. I want to chalk it up to that, because if it's something else, something more sinister, then maybe Karen is right. Maybe I am being duped. And by more than one person.

Anna's house is bustling with people; her husband is on the covered porch in the backyard with another man I recognize from Anna's social circle. They're drinking beer and talking about the game, and Ruthie and Olive run to the chickens where a few other kids are hanging out. It's pouring down rain, but the kids are running around happy, so I don't mind. I see the assistant, Marley, who was here the other morning and give her a quick wave before sidling up next to Anna in the kitchen, asking if there is anything I can do to help. She's pulling a cookie sheet of glazed chicken wings from the oven and points to a head of celery. "Cut that up?"

I nod, grabbing a knife from the butcher block as she begins to launch into a story about a fight she had with Elle.

"She was the one who asked if I wanted the business. It was her idea. Now she's getting all weird about it. Like, why say you'll sign paperwork if you aren't going to?"

"So it's not official?" I ask. "The other day you made it seem like it was a done deal."

"Well, good as done," Anna says as she uses tongs to move the chicken wings to a platter. "But nothing is going to change. We would keep the corporate office, we'd stay the course with the product line. It's not a big deal."

I laugh. "Just the small fact that you'd be the CEO."

Anna grins, opening a jar of organic blue cheese dressing. The label makes me smile, thinking of the conversation with the girls yesterday. "Yes, that small thing."

Just then, there is a knock on the front door. "Come in," Anna calls, wiping her hands on a dishtowel. "It must be Henry and Jolene from the city council," she says breezily as she fluffs her hair, walking to the foyer. As I arrange the celery on the platter, I can't help but overhear the conversation.

"I'm sorry, what do you want?" Anna says coldly. "You must be mistaken."

"No, ma'am," a man says. "We're sorry to disrupt your party. But we need you to come with us. You can either come voluntarily or we'll be forced to bring you in."

"It's the Super Bowl," Anna argues. "I have artichoke dip on the stove." She's coming through the house, to the kitchen, eyes wild. "Gray, say something to them. Explain that I have company. That I can't come now."

Two police officers follow Anna and I recognize them both. Officer Truce, who was called to the scene when I found Patrick, and Boone. His eyes flit over to mine, and he frowns, meeting Truce's gaze.

I tense, not liking the way they share a look with one another, indicating something. Someone. Me.

"Look, you can come with us, or we can have this conversation here in front of all your friends," Truce says just as Anna's husband walks in the room.

"What's going on here?" Jasper asks, looking to Anna with wide eyes, caught utterly off guard. As if he has no idea why the Tacoma PD would be interested in speaking with his wife. I used to think he was a solid man, but now I'm questioning everything. Does he even know Anna is buying wELLEness?

"Am I under arrest or something?" Anna asks.

"No, we want to bring you in for questioning. We'd appreciate your cooperation."

"But the game," Jasper says as if that is relevant to anything.

My eyebrows lift and I feel sick to my stomach. The men at Garden Temple were fools, but maybe all men are.

I walk out the back door and call for my girls. It's time for us to go.

CHAPTER 17

The next day as I'm getting the girls' lunches packed, I get a text from Anna.

> Anna: *Picking up from last night, I'm really sorry if yesterday scared you.*

> Me: *It's okay. Glad you're home.*

She called last night apologizing for the drama earlier in the day. Apparently she was at the station for three hours and it was a whole ordeal. She said the police interrogated her about where she was the night Patrick was killed and had all sorts of questions about wELLEness. On the phone she'd said, "I don't understand why they don't call Elle. Her name is on the branding."

"But you're the new owner, right?"

"Do I want to be after this? It's all too much, Gray."

When I asked about a service for Patrick, she told me his body still hadn't been released. "They are running toxicology and DNA reports on him. Can you imagine, our Patrick who was uber-obsessed with health, having anything toxic in his system?"

The call had ended with her apologizing again, and now, first thing today, she is back at it. Why is she so concerned about how I feel in this moment? Her brother's killer is still at large.

Anna: *Since I have you, think you could bring Patrick's deliveries to the office this morning? I'm pretty sure you have them?*

Me: *I do. So sorry, totally forgot about it. Everything has been so off. He left them here the day of my party.*

Thinking back to that day is like a gut punch. Patrick had been so excited for me to host my first event, even brought flowers when he came with his drop-offs. Our system was simple; on a bi-monthly basis he would bring the orders to me and I would do the deliveries for him. We'd only done it twice so far, which is partly why I had completely forgotten about the orders waiting for their homes.

Anna: *Oh thank God. I had some emails from Patrick's eager customers. Not as VIP as the marina ladies, but we want to keep them happy. Told them all to come to the wELLEness Center at nine a.m. That work with you?*

Me: *No problem, I'll drop them off on my way to work.*

Anna: *See you then.*

* * *

After the girls get on the bus, I head to the garage. As I open the door I'm reminded of the last wELLEness event I attended. I groan, remembering those awful women, smug and rich and not at all understanding of how heartbreaking this all is.

Turning on the lights, I head to the storage rack that Patrick built for me. But as I step across the concrete floor, water splashes around my feet. Crap, all the rain from the weekend must have accumulated and now there's water everywhere.

Kneeling, careful not to get my jeans wet, I reach for the box closest to me, but the cardboard bottom falls out, sending wELLEness products everywhere.

Not wanting to waste any time, and glad Anna isn't here to see this mess I've made, I quickly gather the ruined items and carry them inside. After setting them on the kitchen counter, I head back out to grab the two boxes that were safely stowed on the rack, therefore undamaged.

It takes thirty minutes to sort through the boxes, figuring out what supplements are water-damaged and who gets what replacement. I'm glad Patrick had the idea to stock the upper shelving in the garage with some of the most popular products in his inventory so I could replace them here without having to travel back to his condo. I am already cutting it close to get to work as it is.

These orders contain lots of the multi-vitamin called enRICHment —these customers have all purchased at least three bottles — though I suppose it is cold and flu season.

Once I've gotten everything organized, I load up my car and head to the center. I throw an extra bottle of enRICHment in my purse because, to be honest, I could use a little tension relief today.

Thankfully there is no traffic, though when I pass a Tacoma PD patrol car, I do feel the itch to crane my neck and see if it's Boone. I wish I knew him better because I am dying to know more about the case, who they have leads on, and if there is any way I can help. I think about the fact he gave me his card the first day we met. But calling him up feels like crossing boundaries, not to mention inviting in trouble.

There is a reason I steer clear of the law, why I have forged documents, why my daughters immunization records have a different last name recorded on them. I can't risk having my name in the headlines, having my children found.

When I get to the center, I park in the garage, then take the elevator to the wELLEness floor. I wave quickly to Treydon at the front desk, then walk to the supply closet for the dolly. Back on the ground floor, I load the boxes from my trunk onto the dolly before heading straight up the way I came.

In the elevator, the doors begin to slide shut when a woman shoves her hands between them and forces her way inside. She presses a hand to her chest as she catches her breath. She is thin, tan, with blonde hair in perfectly messy waves. And eyes that light up the small, enclosed space.

"Oh God, sorry," she says. "I could have just caught the next one. I was just eager to get upstairs."

"Where are you headed?" I ask, pointing to the buttons beside me, indicating the different floors.

"Three, thanks," she says.

"Headed to the same place."

Her bright eyes grow even more brilliant as she looks me over. I wonder what she sees. A woman in a bulky navy peacoat and basic blue jeans. Thrifted brown boots and dollar store gloves.

Or maybe something else, because she clasps her hands together. "You're Gray, aren't you? Patrick's Gray? We didn't meet last time there were deliveries because I was in Tahiti. Needed a yoga retreat like you wouldn't believe. I was so tense, you know?"

I nod slowly, knowing plenty about tension, not so much about exotic trips. "Didn't realize he'd mentioned me."

"Said you were his little lucky charm." She blinks quickly, but I see the tears all the same. "I just can't believe he's gone. It's seems . . . impossible."

"I know," I say softly. "It's all so heartbreaking."

"I'm Claire, by the way. And I'm guessing this box has my order?" She peers over the dolly playfully.

The elevator doors open and she exits, me following with the rolling dolly in front of me. Treydon runs from around his desk and wraps Claire into a big hug. "Oh girl, I've missed you!"

"Did you get my texts?" she asks. "Me and the girls have been so torn up about poor Patrick."

"Thank you, Claire. Means *so* much," Treydon says, his eyes shifting, making me doubt his sincerity.

Anna walks out of one of the offices right then, Elle nowhere in sight. Where has she gotten off to? I wish I knew more about her, where she lives, where she's from — but she has always been so private. Anna smiles warmly at me before greeting Claire.

"Glad you could come in," Anna says. "Everything has been a bit chaotic, as I'm sure you can imagine."

Claire nods with understanding. "Of course. I can't imagine. And not to be insensitive, but are the orders going to return to a normal schedule, with delivering to residences?"

I nod. "Of course, it was a mistake. With everything going on, the deliveries slipped my mind. I will be back to the regular route."

"Oh good," Claire says, pressing her palms in a namaste prayer pose and giving me a slight bow. "I know some of Patrick's regulars will be here any minute for their pickups."

"Well, Treydon will be here to help you all," Anna says.

I look at Treydon. "Thank you," I say. "Hate to run, but I've really got to get to work. Everything is there and ready to go, but call if you have any questions, okay?"

"Of course, so nice to meet you," Claire says.

"Same." Then, turning to Anna, I add. "Call me if you hear anything."

She nods and I turn toward the elevator. As the doors slide closed I swear I hear Treydon lean in and whisper, "*She has no clue.*"

Maybe I'm wrong, hearing things, finding problems where there aren't any.

Or maybe my intuition is more powerful than any of the wELLEness vitamins I'm peddling.

CHAPTER 18

When I get home from work, I realize I left the kitchen a mess this morning when repackaging the boxes and replacing the waterlogged bags of products with new ones. The clock tells me the girls will be home in forty-five minutes, so I get to work on cleaning, knowing once they're home the afternoon will pass in a blur of activity — Ruthie has dance class tonight and we always get tacos at a food truck after. Even in the cold it's fun because they have an enclosed tent with space heaters.

As I reach for a trash bag under the kitchen sink, I hear my cell phone buzz. I grab it, answering the unknown number as I open the garbage bag. "Hello, this is Gray."

"Oh thank God you answered. It's Claire. We met this morning? Anyways, I was just talking with Suze and Lia, they're in my neighborhood and we all ordered from Patrick. Thing is, we're all kind of freaking out."

"About what?" I ask, frowning as I begin to empty the product bags into the trash. The wet brochures and vitamin bottles with the labels peeling off, making them impossible to resell.

"These aren't the enRICHment vitamins we usually get."

"What do you mean?" I ask.

"Look at them, they're all white ovals. Patrick brings us small red pills. The *red pills.*"

"Okay, let me open some and figure this out," I say calmly, not aware of a different variety that are red. I actually can't think of any wELLEness product that is red. We don't use any artificial colors.

I reach for a bottle that I just dumped in the trash bag, and twist off the lid — the plastic seal has been removed. Then, frowning at the fact there is no ball of cotton pressed against the supplements, I pour the contents of the bottle out onto the counter.

They are all red. Bright red.

"Okay, just a sec, let me check my storage," I say, walking to the garage. I jump over a puddle and grab a plastic tote bin on the middle shelf with my extra product — the product I used to replace the ruined ones from Patrick this morning. I pull out two bottles of enRICHment and head back to the kitchen, opening one of them as I walk. White ovals. The stuff I have here is all what I expect. I look at the pills on the counter. The ones from Patrick are different.

The bottles I have in my stockpile are all from the corporate distribution center. Patrick's bottles were all opened before being given to me.

My stomach twists in knots as I realize the supply chain was tampered with. Patrick got product from wELLEness but somewhere along the line they became something different. They became tiny red pills.

"Are you still there?" Claire asks. "Do you think we can meet up? Really need my pills. So do my girlfriends. Like now."

"I don't have any red pills," I lie. "I'm sorry, I think there must have been some miscommunication somewhere along—"

The call goes dead. Claire hung up on me midsentence.

I pick up a red pill. One side is marked with a 60, the other side OP. I have no idea what it is, but it's valuable enough that Patrick was the only one who handled them, and he never told me he was switching product out. I wonder if he was doing this with more than enRICHment? There's no way for me to know, considering I just dropped off all of Patrick's latest orders. If he tampered with anything else, it isn't in my hands.

I count fourteen of the bottles of enRICHment with waterlogged labels, and as I quickly uncap them, I see they all have the red pills. Which means everyone in today's delivery was in on whatever Patrick was doing.

I think of the marina ladies, Patrick's VIP customers. Did I bring them these pills too? And what are they? Drugs?

I shove all the empty bottles into the trash, and carry it to the garbage can next to the house. Then I take the pile of red pills and fill a gallon Ziplock baggie with them before taking it to my bedroom, and shoving it in my drawer. I don't want to throw them out and have them accidentally get in the wrong hands. I can't flush them down the toilet not knowing what they contain.

With the house still empty, I pull out my laptop — the one Patrick gifted me — and open the spreadsheet of Patrick's VIP clients. I know there are more than the marina ladies. Higher tiers than the drop-offs I do, clients who buy more than Claire and her neighbors. The spreadsheet has the clients differentiated by how much they order in an average month, over the last year. I count twenty-six clients who spend more than five thousand dollars a month on wELLEness products.

That is a lot of vitamins no matter how you cut it.

They are the big-time buyers, and the ones who have Patrick at the top ranks of wELLEness, or at least had him there. Did they all receive product that was tampered with? Is this why they bought product in the first place? And what exactly are the red pills?

Opening a web browser, I type in "OP 60 Red Pill".

And immediately am faced with hundreds of results. Unanimously telling me the same thing. The pills in the baggie are Oxycontin 60mg ER tablets.

"Oxycodone belongs to a class of drugs known as opioid analgesics. It works in the brain to change how your body feels and responds to pain."

Opioids.

I close the laptop, wanting to scream. How can I reconcile the Patrick I knew with the person who tricked me into making drug drop-offs for him?

The front door opens and Olive calls for me. "Mom? We're home!"

Not having time to decide what to do about all of this, I go downstairs to greet my daughters. Wanting them to believe everything is fine, everything is absolutely normal.

The last thing I want them to know is that their mother has been played by another man. Only this time I've been duped into delivering drugs.

CHAPTER 19

The girls are oblivious to the anger building beneath my surface. Not wanting to be home, I ask if they want to get an after-school treat. I think of the coffee shop I went to the other day, knowing they would love a holiday-themed drink. "And then we can do some window shopping before dance class. I think someone has a birthday coming up soon," I say with a smile.

Ruthie jumps up and down, "Really, Mom?"

Olive looks at me dubiously, knowing this is as out of character as anything. "What's going on?"

"Nothing," I say, my voice an octave higher than normal. "Just want to spend quality time with my daughters."

Ten minutes later I have Ruthie's dance clothes in a canvas bag, and a few books — one for Olive, one for me, to entertain ourselves with during the class.

It's drizzling as we get in the car and I take a deep breath as I drive out of our neighborhood toward the always bustling downtown. For a moment I'm scared I might start crying, so frustrated with myself for falling for Patrick.

Not as a lover, but as a friend. I let him sweet talk me the same way I let Jeremiah get me to trust him so long ago.

"What aren't you saying?" Olive asks, looking over at me as I look for a parking space.

"Nothing," I say, reaching for her hand and squeezing. I place my hands back on the wheel a moment later and it's a good thing because I slam on my breaks as I nearly miss the stop sign. "Sorry," I say, shaking my head. I need to get a grip; the last thing I want right now is a ticket. I already feel way too close to breaking the law. Technically I probably have. Was each wELLEness delivery another violation?

I can't think about that right now. The girls are pointing to an empty parking spot and I pull in, glad to be off the road.

When we get inside the coffee shop, I do a double take. Sitting at a table, with an open newspaper, is Boone. Of course he's here. Not wanting him to notice me, I scoot the girls forward, into line, and the girls both order a Vanilla Valentine Hot Chocolate and I order the Lavender Love Latte.

"Can we have them here, Mom?" Olive asks. "It's so cute inside."

"Would you like mugs then?" the barista asks. Olive asserts herself and tells her yes.

Part of me wants to get the heck out of here because whenever I'm around Boone I feel off-kilter in a way I've never known before. But the other part of me is happy to oblige my daughter, and pleased that Olive asked for what she wanted. That is what I want my girls to be capable of. Making their needs known, not kowtowing to those of other people. Other men.

When the drinks are ready, we take our mugs topped with handmade marshmallows and look for a table. Ruthie runs over to the one by the window, mesmerized by the snowflakes in the window display, and of course, it is directly next to Boone's.

"Oh, I know you," Olive says. "You're that cop who was over."

Boone's eyes lift, looking my daughters over, then letting them land on me. He gives me a wry smile, the kind of look only a man who knows exactly who he is can give. "Back for more perfume masked as a latte?"

I smile. "Yes, and let me guess, you're drinking plain coffee?"

He shakes his head. "No, I got fancy. Ordered a Vanilla Valentine."

"Me too!" Ruthie says, grinning. "We're twins."

Olive and I sit down at our table while Ruthie walks to the window, tracing the snowflakes with her fingertip.

"So why aren't you out arresting people?" Olive asks.

"Everyone needs a coffee break every once in a while." Boone runs a hand over his jaw. He's in a suit, the only thing I've ever seen him in, and it's rumpled, like he pulled it from a pile of clothes. I wonder what else he needs a break from. There are circles under his eyes, the scruff on his jaw is turning into a beard and he looks exhausted.

"You doing okay?" I ask, turning my chair toward him. I hand Olive my phone and she begins taking photos of her hot cocoa, and then of Ruthie's.

"Honestly?" he scratches the back of his head. "No. This case is killing me."

"You're not any closer?"

He shakes his head, ever so slightly. "Maybe it's the weather. Been a cloud hanging over us all week, the rain. It's hard to feel like there is ever gonna be a crack of light."

"I know. My garage has an inch of water after the rainfall this weekend."

Boone frowns. "You have someone to help you with that?"

For a moment I wonder if he is going to offer and I sit back up, straighter in my chair. Scared of him inching closer to me. But I clearly read him wrong because a moment later he clears his throat and says, "I know a good plumber if you need one is all."

"No, it happens all the time, it's no big deal."

"Right, of course." He picks up his mug and takes a drink. I do too, looking at the photo Olive is showing me. She's now taking pictures of a lady with dogs outside. A pair of basset hounds who look miserable in the cold.

"I wish we had a dog," she sighs.

"You ever had one?" Boone asks.

Olive smiles. "Yeah. Lazarus. He was a big old lab but he was loyal. Followed us everywhere."

"Sorry you lost him," Boone says, thinking he is following along.

I tense as Olive opens her mouth. "Oh, he's still alive. He lives with our dad is all." Then she darts a look at me, as if realizing she has said the exact wrong thing.

Boone, though, doesn't pay any mind. Which I suppose makes sense; he knows the girls came from somewhere.

"Where does Lazarus live?" he asks, nonchalant as a detective. Okay, so he did notice.

"In uh, um." Her lips twitch.

I jump in. "In Spokane," I say. "We used to live there."

"Oh yeah?" Boone lights up. "I went to college at Eastern Washington University. Where about did you live?"

Not wanting to get into any more personal territory with Boone, I try to think of the easiest way to get out of this conversation. I decide to be honest because in truth I know very little about that city.

"It wasn't actual Spokane. It was closer to Moses Lake."

"Oh yeah?" Boone nods slowly. "Pretty small town, right? Big difference from Tacoma."

"I like the city. Had enough small town life for a lifetime."

Boone laughs. "Then you wouldn't like Buckley, where I live. But I do have a dog, his name is Matisse."

"What color is he?" Ruthie asks.

Boone pulls out his phone and on the lock screen is a French bulldog — the exact opposite of what I would imagine a gruff guy like Boone owning.

"He's so cute!" Ruthie squeals. "I want to meet him."

"Yeah, and the thing about Frenchies is they don't need lots of walks. He just sits by the front window all day watching the birds fly around."

"Well, I wanna walk him," Ruthie says with a toothy grin.

Matisse. A famous French painter who used vibrant colors and bold designs. I know that because I sometimes look through art books while I'm on my lunch break at the library. It's not the name I would think this gruff detective would have chosen. Then again, what do I know about Boone, really?

What do any of us know about one another at all? Clearly I didn't know Patrick.

The girls have finished their drinks and I tell them it's time to go. Boone stands, shrugging. "I should go too. Gotta case to crack."

Olive looks up at him solemnly. "Patrick's case?" she asks softly.

Boone's eyes meet mine. I nod, ever so slightly. "Don't worry," Boone says, setting a hand on her shoulder. "We got lots of officers working on it."

"Do you think the person who killed him might kill again?" she asks.

Boone shakes his head, adamant. "No. That isn't going to happen. It's my job to make sure it doesn't."

His words, though, don't sound like a promise, they sound like fear.

CHAPTER 20

At Ruthie's dance class, I try to read the novel I packed. It's the story of a paper bride, sent from China to San Francisco, a woman taking on her dead sister's life as her own to gain entrance and a chance at a brighter future.

But it's hard to focus. Every time the main character begins to doubt her decision to leave behind the only world she knew for a better life, I'm brought to the past, doubting my choices, too.

The lobby of the dance studio is full of parents, mostly mothers, on their phones or tablets, trying to pass the hour more quickly. I wonder if the people around me have pasts they want to forget about too.

Uncovering the fact that Patrick had used me in his con made me feel like a fool. And it brings me back to when I was young, fourteen and so vulnerable. Able to be molded into whatever was needed of me. An orphan, with an aunt and uncle who had been drinking the Garden Temple Kool-Aid for years, without any concern for my wellbeing, or assuming that marrying the prophet — their most holy man — was a blessing for me. For them.

When I left Garden Temple I swore to myself I would never be a victim again, never be at the mercy of someone else, someone else's teaching — but didn't I buy into everything Patrick promised? Is that any different than Jeremiah? Maybe worse even, because I have a gallon-sized baggie of opiates in my underwear drawer.

The novel in my lap features a bride who knew what she was walking into on her wedding day. I, on the other hand, had no clue.

When I joked with my neighbors about my wedding night a week ago while our kids decorated cookies, I wasn't exaggerating my pleasure during our first time. When we married, I was in love with Jeremiah. Lust at least. Maybe I didn't quite believe that a man could actually be a direct line to God, but I did believe in Jeremiah's power, his influence. He was handsome and tall, with strong arms and strong convictions. And he saw me at my very, very worst and told me he would keep my secret forever. He offered me his hand in marriage, burying my secret and giving me an alternative I so badly craved.

It wasn't until later that I realized what my life was. What it was to become. At fourteen years old I was pregnant and completely reliant on a man who was intent on bending my will to his. At the time, he was fifteen years older than me, the age I am now. To do what he did to me, a child, it's unfathomable.

It's moments like this I wonder if I'm a monster. For not telling the police the absolute truth. But if I do that, I fear my sister wives will lose their children — that something terrible will happen, like all the kids at the compound entering foster care. I remember women at the compound mentioning what happened to the Fundamentalist Mormons in Texas — after they were raided, fifty-two girls were sent into foster care. I can't take Lydia and Naomi's children from them. I can't.

And beyond that, I can't go to jail and lose my daughters. Jeremiah has proof to send me there. And if he finds me, he could easily make an anonymous tip that could destroy everything I've built for the girls.

So I'm stuck, being quiet, still.

At our wedding Jeremiah lifted my veil and made an oath to protect me forever. Standing before the man we called Prophet, I heeded his words. And I wanted protection. Especially after what had happened only days before. I wanted to believe that he was honest and good, that he wanted to keep his word.

It wasn't until later, after Abel was born, that I truly began to realize how small my world was and always would be.

When I was a girl, when my parents were still alive, I had dreams, plans. I was going to be a florist. I remembered my dad bringing my mom flowers for her birthday, their anniversary — Valentine's Day — and I thought it was the most magical thing, how my mom's face would break into a big smile, how she'd wrap her arms around his neck and give him a kiss, oohing and ahhing over the arrangement. It made their love blossom, those flowers, and I thought it was the prettiest thing in the world — the smile on my mom's face when he gave them to her. I wanted to be a part of that sort of joy.

On my wedding day I had one request of my aunt, and she fulfilled it. I dressed in a long white gown, simple and modest, a long veil trailing behind me. She handed me the bouquet I dreamed about, wishing then for my mom to be giving them to me, for my father to be walking me down the aisle.

I blink back tears now, at the memory, flipping the pages of the book and pretending it's the story in my hands that has me emotional, not the memories of my own life.

I haven't become a florist, obviously. I shelve books with my head lowered, I say little to my coworkers and keep things at surface level, polite. The only people I've let in are Anna and Patrick and now . . . now I wonder why I let that happen.

I was lonely, sure. Desperate for company because even though my sister wives drove me up the wall nearly every day, they were family. They knew I loved my waffles extra crispy, that my favorite tea was lavender chamomile, that I was an early bird, never a night owl. They knew me. Jeremiah knew me too.

He knew I was scared of driving in the car too fast, scared of his temper, scared of his punishments for the kids and his wives. Penance, he called it, and he made us pay. He knew my fears and used them against me, telling me it was time for a driving lesson and then he would take the driver's seat, accelerating until I was begging him to stop, tears streaking my cheeks, fear twisted up inside of me. Memories of the car crash that took the lives of my parents. Praying this drive wouldn't take ours.

Now, in the present, in the lobby of Ruthie's ballet class, Olive takes my hand in hers. It's not until she places her hand on my back that I realize I'm shaking, reliving the past in a way that has me showing more of myself than I want.

"Mom," Olive whispers. "Mom, you need fresh air."

She takes my book and sets it aside, pulling me to stand, and pushing open the doors of the lobby.

I take in lungfuls of ice-cold air, leaning against the brick building as Olive stares at me, panicked.

"Is it because of me?" she asks.

"What?" I gasp.

She bites her bottom lip. "I thought you were mad at me for mentioning Dad. I'm sorry, Mom. I know I shouldn't have. I promised I wouldn't but it just spilled out and I couldn't take it back, it was too late."

I pull Olive to me. "No, sweetheart, you did nothing wrong. You're perfect."

"Then why are you so upset?"

I kiss the top of her hair, knowing that I made the right choice, even if it's scary, even if it's hard. I had to take my daughters away from that place. I just wish I hadn't introduced them to another man who had such bad intentions. Bad intentions for me.

I need to know who killed Patrick. He is not the man I thought he was.

Now that I know I was dealing his drugs, I'm scared. Because what if now someone comes after me too?

CHAPTER 21

In the middle of the night I hear a noise. I wake with a start to the sound.

Sitting up, I clench my fists, trying to focus on the sound. But there is a buzzing of fear in my ear.

He's found us.

Is it a click of the back door? The garage opening?

The sound has me jumping from bed, my bare feet on the cold hardwood floors, and I think of the last year, of the growth I've made with the girls. My heart races with the thought of leaving this home for Garden Temple.

Has Jeremiah come to take us back? Is he only taking the girls?

I can't lose them. Tears prick the corners of my eyes at the thought, but I blink them away, forcing myself to take one step, then another, tiptoeing to the landing, listening. There isn't any sound to follow.

I race down the stairs, run to the kitchen. It's empty. But as I move to the window over the kitchen sink I see a dark figure running through the yard. Tall, lean. His back is to me.

My first instinct is to assume it's Jeremiah running away, but there's another thought in the forefront of my mind, and it only intensifies as I realize the door leading from the garage into the house is open. I didn't do that, did I?

And there is one very good reason why someone would want to be in my garage right now. And it has nothing do with the secondhand lawnmower or rake. It has everything to do with the stash of wELLEness product stored there.

What if it is someone after the drugs? The ones stored in my dresser drawer.

Someone who hasn't gotten what they wanted. Needed. Someone with motive to kill.

Maybe it wasn't Jeremiah who shot Patrick in cold blood . . . because as much as I felt motive pointed to him at first, now I have my doubts. This seems to be bigger than my husband looking for me.

If he knew where I was, wouldn't he confront me? Take the girls? It isn't like Jeremiah to stand by knowing someone opposes him. He is a man who takes action to get what he wants.

I've been foolish thinking it was Jeremiah — I've been too single-minded. All I wanted was to stay under the radar but my need for extra money has exposed me. Has compromised the girls.

I flick on the light near the garage door, wanting to see if there's any indication that someone was in here, rifling through the product. But I had already made a mess of things earlier when I was rooting in the bins, looking for replacements.

Frustrated, I turn off the light and lock the door. As I triple check the front and back door locks, my whole body feels tight with worry. On the kitchen counter is another glass Coke bottle.

Is Jeremiah torturing me?

I shudder as I pick it up, the glass a cruel joke. Clear when everything feels so cloudy. Someone was in my house — my home. The violation I feel winds up my spine and I need to see my girls, see that they are safe.

I walk upstairs and pause at the cracked open doorways of my daughters. They are sleeping deeply, blissfully unaware of the trauma that threatens to surface.

As I get back in bed, I try to play out which scenario is better. But they are both impossible. A drug dealer looking for their product or a cult leader looking for respect?

* * *

In the morning Ruthie is in my bed before I've even gotten up, asking for French braids. "The fancy kind, Mom. There's a party today!"

I smile, remember it is Valentine's Day, refusing to let the nightmares I chased for hours threaten today. "Of course, do you have those red ribbons from Christmas? I can thread them through."

She jumps down the bed and runs back to her room and I rub under my eyes, wanting to be fully present for the next hour until the girls get on the school bus.

In the kitchen I make heart-shaped pancakes and even cut their peanut butter and jelly sandwiches into the same shape. I remember my own mother doing this for me, and it feels like a miracle to be here, without sister wives looking over my shoulder, judging me for my parenting choices. I add chocolate kisses to the lunch boxes, even though I know they will be loaded up with sugar at school today.

"You got all your cards?" I ask them as they tug on their backpacks. Olive nods, holding up a canvas tote bag to prove it.

"Kids at school might think this is dorky, that we made them all."

But Ruthie shakes her head emphatically. "No, Olive. They will think they are the most specialest. Handmade is always best, I promise." She's younger, but talks like she's wiser, and I smile, finding it adorable.

I walk them to the bus stop, even though Olive says I don't need to. "We're fine, Mom."

But they don't know the worry etched in my heart after last night's intruder. It may be Valentine's Day, a date marked for love — but I feel a growing sense of danger with each step I take.

Anna is giving me a lot of reasons to doubt her intentions. I need to talk to Karen again. Maybe she knows more than she let on. Maybe she knows something about Patrick and Anna's relationship that I don't.

As we walk to the bus stop, a new neighbor, Granger, waves hello. He's a man not much older than me who moved in a few weeks ago, and he's outside, getting the newspaper. The three of us wave back. Another door down is Avery, who is just setting out from her house with her twins in a jogging stroller. At the bus stop, Kendall is trying to smooth down her son's hair, and she tells the girls they look so cute all dressed up.

The bus pulls up and I tell them I love them, my anxiety fading as I walk back to my house. This neighborhood is safe and I am creating a small safety network for my girls. If we are ever in trouble, there are plenty of people here to look out for us.

On my way to work, I make the decision to stop at Save N Clip. Karen made it clear she had no good will toward Patrick, but why, specifically? She called her manager over to ask about sale prices the other morning, cutting our conversation short. I need to finish it.

Once again, the store is nearly empty when I enter. This time I forgo the shopping cart and head straight to Karen's register. She's typing on her phone, and doesn't notice me at first. When I say her name, she slides her phone into her apron and rolls her eyes.

"What?" she huffs. "I didn't have the energy to deal with Patrick's bullshit when he was alive, I certainly don't when he's dead."

"I know you have a lot on your plate," I say. "But I need to know why you think he's a con artist."

"He knew I was in a tough spot, and preyed on my desperation. I'm guessing you have a sob story too?"

I flinch, thinking I do a good job of protecting myself. But maybe my facade is a lot more transparent than I want to believe.

"Look," Karen says. "He tells you he can help you make a ton of cash, fast, but it's a scam. No one except those at the top are making enough money to pay bills. God knows I can sell the shit out of stuff. But it didn't matter how many face masks and essential oils I bought for Christmas gifts or sold to the ladies on the PTA. I was never able to pay off a single hospital bill for Sonny even after hustling for Patrick for a year. But you know what kinda money he made? Enough for a vacation in Brazil. A new car. A fancy electric one. You know what I drive? A Toyota Corolla." Karen rolls her eyes. "He's a scammer, all of them are. You know that Elle lady gets Botox? Her skin does *not* look like that because of upLIFT, I can tell you that right now."

"So it's just the business model that has you upset with him?" I ask, wanting to know if she had any idea about the prescription pills getting dealt in the vitamin packaging.

She scoffs. "Just? God, that is no business model. It's a pyramid scheme, plain and simple. You know I was invited to another home party a week or so back?" She pulls out her phone, tapping on the Facebook app. She scrolls before landing on what she's looking for. "Look here, can you believe it? A friend from high school is selling jewelry in the same way. Went to her party but this stuff was all cheap crap. Look."

She hands me the phone and I see Karen with a few other ladies, sitting on a couch, jewelry displayed on the coffee table in front of them. Just like the home party I threw the night Patrick was killed.

I look at the photo. Everyone in it is tagged, and it's dated with a timestamp even.

It is the same night as my party. The same night Patrick was left in a pool of his own blood.

"How long was the party?" I ask.

She shrugs. "I got there at six, only expected to stay an hour, but then Tara opened some wine and made pizza rolls and next thing I knew it was nine-thirty." She laughs. "That's how these businesses get ya, you know? Just some ladies looking for something fun, next thing ya know, the garage is full of jewelry from China or leggings from Taiwan and you have nothing but merchandise you can't get rid of."

Knowing that Karen's alibi is airtight, I hand her back the phone. "I'm sorry this all happened to you, Karen."

"I just hope you are smarter than me. Get out before you've sunk ten grand you don't have into someone else's company."

The figure shocks me. "Ten grand?"

She nods. "Yeah, hard lesson learned. Never trust anyone who isn't family."

I thank her again, and leave the store. Wishing her words rang more true. Trouble with family is that sometimes they can't be trusted either.

CHAPTER 22

When I get off work I see a voicemail left twenty minutes ago from a number I don't recognize. When I get in my car, I turn it on, needing the heat to defrost the windshield. I press play, listening to the message.

"Hey, Gray. It's Elle. I need you to call me. It's important. Thanks, love."

I call her back right away, having never spoken to her on the phone in my life, but praying as it rings that she has new information on what happened to Patrick.

"Hey, it's Gray," I say. "You called?"

"Can you come over? I'd really like to touch base with you."

"At the center?"

"Actually, no," Elle says. "Can you come to my place? I live in Dash Point. I'll text you the address."

"Sure," I say, looking at my clock. "I'll see you soon." The girls will be out of school in twenty minutes so I give Luna a quick call. "Hey," I say when she picks up right away. "I was wondering if you were busy this afternoon?"

After explaining things, she quickly agrees to meet the girls at the bus stop and let them hang out with her until I get home. "And no rush," Luna says. "I hope you get some clarity on what happened to your friend."

Feeling relieved to have a small network of friendships, I enter Elle's address into the GPS on my phone and begin the route.

The drive isn't long, but as I wind around the water, it is impossible not to marvel at the view. Mount Rainier hovers above us, a snowy peak glittering in the sky, the majestic blue water of Puget Sound surrounding us — it's breathtaking. All those years in church, reading about God's creation, this is what the Bible was talking about. This is the sort of beauty I missed all those years living amidst the dusty tumbleweeds of eastern Washington. There, the summer heat burned the ground, the land as parched as I was. I missed the mountain ranges of my childhood, the ferry boat rides across the deep water of the sound. I may not have grown up in Tacoma, but the views make me feel like I've returned home.

Elle lives in a large waterfront mansion with a sleek and modern design. Slate and granite slabs lean against one another, serving as architectural art in the front yard, the massive front doors of imperial red, and a rock garden to the left of the house is a Zen masterpiece. I knock tentatively, not knowing what to expect from a woman as wealthy as Elle. Did her money come from her company or from selling drugs?

When the doors swing open I'm welcomed into her embrace. "You found us," she says. Her ethereal beauty sweeps me up as she leads me deeper inside her home. Treydon is here, sitting on a white leather couch, flanked by statues that look like they've been transported from a Buddhist monastery. Religious figures, gilded in gold, in meditative poses. There are several large yucca trees in massive pots, a living wall covered in plants with trailing vines, and a succulent display on a circular coffee table that could grace the cover of a magazine. Then I realize it actually has — Elle's home must have been used for the photoshoot for last month's wELLEness catalogue.

"You made it," Treydon says, pulling me into a hug. His eyes are rimmed in red and he has large dark circles under them. His usually collected appearance is frayed, and I squeeze him an extra moment, hating to see him so torn up, but understanding the pain. Losing someone is never easy.

"Have the police found Patrick's killer?" I ask, sitting next to him on the leather couch. Elle kneels before us and reaches for the ceramic pot on a side table, pouring three mugs of steaming tea.

"Not yet," Elle says. Then, pausing, she adds. "How well do you know Anna?"

The question catches me off guard. "Pretty well. She is the reason I know Patrick. Why I started helping him with his business."

"And why you became a distributor?" Elle asks.

I nod. "Yes. But I just started selling. My first party was the night Patrick died." I take a sip of the tea. "Why do you want to know about Anna's and my relationship?"

"Well, to be completely transparent," Elle says. "Anna has been telling people that she's buying the company from me, Gray. It's very confusing considering it was never for sale."

I try to remember the conversation I had with Anna on her back porch. She distinctly told me she was taking over wELLEness. Then the morning of the Super Bowl, before the police brought her in for questioning, she mentioned getting in a huge fight with Elle. I know Anna has been behaving oddly, especially in relation to her concern over her brother's killer, but I don't exactly want to tell all of this to Elle — because my alliance lies with Anna. She is the one who helped me get my home; she was the first person in this city to feel like a friend.

On the other hand, her brother Patrick lied to me. He was using me to peddle his drugs. I still have the stash in my underwear drawer.

I don't know who is only telling me half-truths, but Karen's words of warning are heavy on my mind. I feel like multiple people are trying to dupe me. But with what, and why?

"Why would she lie about that?" I ask. "About becoming the new owner of wELLEness?"

Elle and Treydon exchange a look. "That is actually what we were hoping you could help us with, Gray. You know Anna better than we do."

"I haven't even known her a year."

Elle nods slowly. "I understand, but my relationship with her has always been purely professional. Your connection has been more intimate. We thought perhaps you might know why she is acting so erratic."

"Have you spoken to the police?" I ask them. "About any of this? If she isn't being truthful about becoming the owner then maybe there are other cracks in her story," I say, my words tumbling out. But I immediately regret them. I don't want to implicate anyone until the facts are made more clear.

"The police were here earlier, actually," Elle says coolly.

I wonder if Boone was here with them. I'm assuming as the detective on the case he would have been the one questioning Elle.

"The detective actually had some rather unique concerns," Elle says. "Shocking, really."

"Like what?" I swallow. Maybe I should go to the police right now with the bag of red pills. Tell them how I came to have them in my possession. I know it would be the right thing to do.

But the right thing for whom? Not my daughters, surely? If I go to the police they will want my legal name. They will look at my forged ID and fake Social Security card and know I am hiding something. Probably lots of somethings.

And why would they believe that I didn't know about the prescription drugs I was passing around town? Patrick set me up to take the fall. And with him gone, I would.

I can't.

Treydon rests his elbows on his knees. "They were asking Elle about drugs," he says. "Prescription pills."

I tense, but refuse to let my fear show. I don't know either Treydon or Elle well enough to let my guard down, to tell them the truth about what I found in my garage.

I may not have experience with the law, but I know plenty about hiding your emotions, remaining a blank canvas so the people around you can't use your pain or your joy against you.

So your husband can't.

Jeremiah may have been a monster in many ways, but there was so much to learn from his cruelty. How to protect myself was my number one lesson. I didn't have control over how hard he slapped me, couldn't control his anger or rage, his demands. But I could control my response.

"Why?" I ask plainly. "Why ask you about drugs?"

"I'm not sure," Elle says, her face so wrinkle-free it is impossible to know how she truly feels. But then she begins to cry, her shoulders shaking, her face in her hands. "I built this business from nothing. And the idea that I would be doing something illegal . . . it's unfathomable. I want to know what Anna knows, but I can't talk to her."

"Why not?" I ask.

"Because she is trying to take away my baby."

"Baby?"

Treydon rubs Elle's back. "wELLEness has been like a child to her. She has given it her whole life," he explains. "Now Anna is trying to steal it, and someone is talking to the police and mentioning prescription pills."

"Who would do that?" I ask, thinking how only minutes ago I was considering doing the exact same thing.

"You really don't know?" Elle asks, wiping her eyes. "You don't know anything about pills?"

I shake my head. "I'm so sorry this is happening," I say, not lying outright. "I wish I could be of more help."

"It's all right," Elle says. "Thank you for coming over."

I stand, wanting to leave, not wanting to get caught in this any more than I already am. When will the police knock on my door, questioning me?

"I'm heading out too," Treydon says and together we walk to the door. He gives Elle a long hug, and I give her a quick one, awkwardly. “Call if you hear anything,” he tells her.

When we get to the driveway, alone, Treydon takes my hand. “Can you talk?” he asks, urgency in his voice. “It’s about Patrick. I know something no one else knows.”

CHAPTER 23

I text Luna in the car, saying the meeting is turning into dinner and asking if she'd mind keeping the girls another few hours.

Luna: *Take your time. We're making Valentine pizza!*

She attaches a photo of my girls and hers around a kitchen island with homemade pizza dough spread out on cookie sheets.

Crap.

Me: *I totally forgot the holiday. I can come back. I don't want to ruin your plans.*

Luna: *Toby has a night shift at the hospital. Gone til the weekend. Our romantic dinner will wait! Honestly, no worries!*

Deciding to take her words at face value, I drive to downtown Tacoma to a brewery Treydon suggested we meet at.

The restaurant is packed, of course it is. It's Valentine's Day. But we manage to find a seat in the bar, and he orders a pilsner and nachos.

"Sparkling water is fine," I tell the waiter. When he leaves, I cut to the chase. "Why didn't you want to talk at Elle's?"

"Because she's a drama queen. Did you not witness her mini meltdown back there?"

"She didn't have a meltdown. She was crying. Which is a reasonable reaction when everything is basically caving in around you."

Treydon frowns, leaning back on his stool. When the waiter brings the drinks, he thanks him, then takes a long drink before speaking. "Look, Gray, I like you. Patrick liked you. Which is why I need to be honest with you before anything comes out about this."

I lace my fingers together, setting my hands on the tabletop, preparing myself for some new information that will change my perspective on all of this. "What is it?"

"Patrick and I were in love."

My eyes grow wide — not because the two men were in love, though my family at Garden Temple would have had issues with this — my surprise comes from the fact I knew nothing about it. I thought Patrick was my closest friend yet he never even hinted at a relationship with Treydon.

I clear my throat. "You were in love?"

Treydon nods. "Yes, and if the police find out, they'll discover that Patrick and I had been together on and off for some time."

"On and off?" I ask, looking for clarity.

The nachos come and Patrick begins eating with gusto. I'm guessing in order to avoid the uncomfortable nature of the conversation, but he was the one who started it. I think of my girls, how I've been gone all day and just want to get home.

"Look, why do you want me to know this?" I ask. "How does this help anything?"

Treydon runs a hand through his receding hair line. "Look, there are some text messages that might look a bit . . . alarming. We weren't exactly nice to one another."

Feeling exhausted by the idea of another man wrapping me up in his drama, I reach for my purse, ready to go.

"I have two kids who need me. If you and Patrick were in an abusive relationship, I sincerely hope you can find the help you need. It's a lot to recover from, I know. But I'm not your safe person, Treydon."

He reaches for my hand. "Don't go. Just listen. Please. I don't have anyone else."

His words pull at my heartstrings, someone saying they are out of options. I've been there. I understand desperation. But I also don't want to be one step closer to Patrick's murderer than I need to be. I have my own interest to protect.

"Anna isn't your friend," he says. Those words keep me seated across from him. With my purse in my lap I wait for him to continue. "She thinks you're more than naive. She thinks you're easy to manipulate."

"Why are you telling me this?" I ask.

"Because I am your friend. No one else in this company is looking out for you. Patrick wasn't."

I narrow in on his words. I have reason to believe Patrick conned me, but does Treydon know to what extent?

"What does that mean?"

He smirks. "It means he could have been paying you a hell of a lot more for what you were doing for him than he ever did."

I want to ask if he's referencing the drugs I was delivering on Patrick's behalf but I also don't exactly want to own up to knowing any of that right now. Not when I don't have any reason to trust Treydon.

"I only worked for Patrick for a month. Hardly long enough for a raise."

Treydon runs a hand over the back of his neck. "God, I'm just so tense. It's too much. The man I loved is dead."

"Why was it a secret?" I ask, thinking of the photo of Patrick, Treydon and I, smashed on his mantel.

"Patrick thought it would upset Elle. She didn't like personal life to mix with business."

"But if you were in love, then wouldn't Elle be happy for you both? Isn't that what wELLEness is all about, becoming the best versions of ourselves?"

Treydon presses his fingers to the bridge of his nose. "That's what I told Patrick. I told him we shouldn't hide our feelings, we should get married, have a family, but he said he wasn't ready."

"And that's why you fought?" I ask.

"Among other things. We saw the business differently too." He rolls his head back, clearly tense.

In my purse I have a tampered-with bottle of enRICH-ment. I had put it in my purse before I realized it was filled with prescription pills. Now, though, it gives me an idea. I'm not interested in my life going backwards. I escaped Garden Temple for freedom, and I won't be a pawn in anyone's game again. It's time for some answers. I need to know who knows what, starting with the man in front of me.

Pulling it out, I unscrew the cap and pour four red pills into my palm. "Here, take these, it will help with your stress."

Treydon's eyes widen and he looks at my hand, then back up to me. "Oh, no, they're yours, I couldn't."

"But this vitamin is chock-full of magnesium," I say tightly. "It will help release your stress right away."

"That's too many," he says, waving a hand to push me off.

"No, the bottle says two to four a day. This is fine, Treydon." I shove them toward him, wanting to push him to the edge.

"Stop it," he seethes. "I don't want those, I can't—"

I put the red pills back in the bottle, screwing the cap back on. "Can't what?" I ask coolly, understanding that Treydon knows exactly what I was offering him and it sure as hell wasn't a wELLEness product. He was in on this, somehow.

I stand up, pulling my purse over my shoulder. "I don't know what you were hoping to get from me, but I won't grant any sympathy to you. I'm done being used by other people, and I won't take the fall for your crimes."

Treydon smiles smugly. "Right, because you have your own crimes to account for, don't you?"

"You know nothing about me," I seethe.

"I know enough, *Grace*. I know plenty."

He knows too much. Everyone does. Backing away, I leave the bar, shook up, tears in my eyes. As I walk outside, into the frigid February air, I run right into Boone. Of course I do.

He's in a flannel shirt and thick wool jacket, his dark eyes meeting mine. An arm around the shoulder of a woman who is blonde and bright, and I have never felt more dull in all my life. Scuffed brown boots and a secondhand heart, worn around the edges, more than bruised.

"Gray?" he asks, worry in his timbre.

"I'm fine," I say, stepping away, toward the sidewalk. I lift my hands as if proving my point. "Please, leave me alone."

I turn, walking to my car, making it clear I don't want to be followed.

And ninety-nine out of a hundred times, I wouldn't want to be. But for some reason, this is the one time I do. But Boone doesn't chase me down, which is probably for the best. Because I am in no place to be caught.

CHAPTER 24

I have the day off from work and the timing couldn't be better. The girls were wound up so tight last night after I got them from Luna's. In part because of the nonstop sugar they had at school for their class parties, but also amped from getting to hang out with Sophie, who is apparently their new best friend. She showed them how to do some TikTok dance. I may not be culturally relevant, but even I realize how meaningful this is for a preteen girl.

However, when they tried to teach me their routine, I drew the line. "How about you show me the moves and then we make some chamomile tea and watch a show?" I'd suggested, too tired to contemplate learning anything. I was already trying to process more information than I knew how to deal with.

This morning, I feel guilty that I didn't just do the dance with them. As I make a pot of coffee in my bathrobe, I try to extend myself grace. But it's hard. At Garden Temple, mothers were taught to always strive to be the best versions of ourselves for our family — no matter the cost.

But that guilt didn't just surface at Garden Temple — it's everywhere. I hear moms of toddlers at the children's section of the library constantly berating themselves to one another for not reading more books aloud, for letting their infant sleep in the swing, for lying down while the baby naps instead of cleaning house. Mothers everywhere are tired, and sometimes I forget that is a normal and healthy reaction to living.

So today I tell myself that I am going to give myself an actual day off.

When Ruthie and Olive bound into the kitchen I know they are surprised to see me still in my bathrobe.

"You're right, Olive, you are old enough to walk yourself and your sister to the bus. Since it's my day off I'm gonna sit in my PJs and drink coffee."

Olive laughs. "Can you imagine what Dad would say?"

I swallow, and Ruthie's eyes widen. She elbows her sister.

"Owww," Olive moans. "Gosh, why can't I say the word Dad? We do have one, you know."

"I know," Ruthie says softly. "But he hurt Mom. A lot. He hurt us too."

"Spare the rod, spoil the child," Olive says, shrugging, repeating the words Jeremiah so often spoke after punishing the children.

Usually, I let Olive's comments slide, not wanting to fight with my girls. But today I can't just let it go.

"Those words are not true," I say sternly. "Your father abused us. He is not a safe man."

"Then why don't we tell that cop, Boone, that Dad should go to jail?" Olive asks.

I falter. "I don't have all the answers, Olive. I'm trying. I'm doing my best. And you are too. But surely, after a year of living in the real world, you've learned that the life you had at Garden Temple was much too small. That you deserve a future bigger and brighter than you could have had there."

She frowns, grabbing a gallon of milk from the fridge and pouring a bowl of cereal. "It would all make sense, except don't Jolene and Sarai deserve a bright future too?"

I nod. "They do. But we can only do one thing at a time. And their moms don't see things the same way as I do."

"They're our sisters though." I see the heartache in her eyes and I hate that tearing her away from the life she has known is doing this, but I also know my job as a mom is to protect my children. Sure, in an ideal world my biggest concern would be mommy guilt over TikTok dances, but our struggles are bigger than that. As much as I wish they weren't.

"I'm sorry, Olive. I'm sorry you are having to go through all of this."

She nods and lets me wrap her in a tight hug. I hold on, not ever wanting to let her go.

I know she feels torn. She is a smart girl, she understands that Garden Temple wasn't a safe place, but she misses it. It was her home. And no matter what age you are, sometimes you just want something familiar.

"So, you never told me last night, did you get any Valentines yesterday?"

She rolls her eyes but Ruthie jumps up and down on one foot. "Tomas gave her a box of chocolate."

"Really?" I smile.

"Mom, please don't make it a thing."

"Why didn't you tell me last night?"

Olive shrugs. "You seemed tired."

"I was, but I always want to hear about your life."

Olive smiles. "Maybe if you aren't too weird about it, I'll share some chocolate after school."

I laugh, appreciating her humor. When they leave for school I feel a sense of calm that is totally unwarranted. There's a killer at large and I have looming fears about their father and am conflicted about what my responsibility is as a citizen, knowing what I know about Garden Temple . . . but in this moment, my twelve-year-old daughter is secure enough to be honest with me, and not just with the easy stuff, with the scary stuff too.

After refilling my coffee cup, I check my phone, opening the *Tacoma Tribune* newspaper app, wishing there was news on Patrick's killer. I slip my phone in my bathrobe pocket and pick up the novel I was finishing at the dance class the other night, about the paper wife. Flipping to my bookmarked page, I settle in. Two hours later I am nearing the final pages of the book, totally sucked into the woman's plight in San Francisco after leaving China. I never thought I would relate in such a startling way to a woman who lived a century ago, but I do. I so often feel misplaced in a world I don't entirely understand.

So absorbed in the book, when I hear a rustling in the garage I startle, dropping the book. Scared.

Closing my eyes, I tell myself to focus, to stay calm. I tiptoe to the garage door off the kitchen and wrap my fingers around the handle. When I pull the door open, I see a man dressed in dark clothes sliding under the garage door that is open just a few feet. Racing to it, I fling it open, running after him. In my slippers and bathrobe, I sprint toward the man. Heart pounding, and clearly out of shape, by the end of the block my hands are on my hips and I am gasping for breath. A car slows, the woman driving looking me over. I wave at her, indicating that I'm okay.

But I'm not.

The phone in my pocket rings. It's a number I don't recognize. "Hello?" I say, answering, my breath still ragged.

"Gray? I need your help."

"Anna, what is it? Where are you?"

"At the police station." Her words are muffled by her sobs, but I can make them out clear enough. But why is she at the station? "Can you come get me?" she asks. "Jasper's out of town. And Patrick's gone and . . ." She's crying harder now.

I look off into the distance. The man in black is slowing his pace, but he's all the way down the hill. Even if I ran home and jumped in my car right now, I wouldn't be able to catch up.

"Of course I can come get you," I say. "I'll be there as soon as I can."

CHAPTER 25

When I get to the station Anna is waiting for me in the lobby. "Thank you, Gray, I didn't know who else to call."

"It's okay," I say slowly as she wraps me into a tight hug. When she pulls back, there are still tears in her eyes. "What happened?"

She's shaken, her eyes darting around. Realizing she wants out of the station, I push open the heavy front doors and we exit. Outside, the air is icy cold, but at least it isn't recycled air.

"Come on," I say. "Let's talk in the car."

A few minutes later we're in my car and driving toward a coffee stand. We order lattes and I drive a few more blocks to a lookout point. With the car in park, and heat on, we face the water.

Anna unbuckles and leans her body toward mine. I match her motions, waiting for her to talk.

"So this morning the cops were back at my house, apparently they had new evidence and wanted to hear what I knew about it."

"What evidence?"

"That's the thing. I honestly don't know. That York guy tiptoed around something for an hour, and the detective,

Boone, was no better. They wouldn't come out and say anything. They wanted me to do the talking. But I didn't know what to say!"

"I saw Elle," I tell her, choosing my words carefully. "And Treydon. She says she never wanted to sell wELLEness."

Anna huffs. "That's not true. I mean, why would I lie about it?"

"I don't know."

Anna's eyes widen. "You think I'm lying about something?"

"Honestly? I don't know, Anna. It's all so sketchy."

"I thought we were friends. I thought you were on my side." She takes a sip of her coffee, then groans, dropping her head on the headrest behind her. "I need some enRICHment so badly. Or BEtterMEnt. My whole body is shaking."

I bite my bottom lip, thinking of last night with Treydon. His reaction when I offered him the red pills. "Oh, I have some, actually." I reach for my purse in the backseat and pull out the enRICHment. I unscrew the cap slowly, wondering when she is going to stop me. I hand her the open bottle, knowing she has high blood pressure. This stimulant could kill her.

She takes the bottle from me and absently begins to pour five of the pills into her palm, her eyes off in the distance as if the weight of the day has been too much for her.

But I'm focused on her and I realize she has no clue what she's about to take. Just when she is about to drop them in her mouth, I grab her wrist. "You have high blood pressure, Anna, you can't take that."

She scrunches up her face. "I know it's a lot of magnesium, but I always take four or five a day. The bottle says four in 24 hours so it's not really that much more, is it?" Registering the shock on my face, she adds, "What? How many of them do you take?"

"It's not that, Anna," I say, knowing that she didn't know about the drugs.

"What is it, then?" She looks at the pills in her hand. "Wait, this isn't what they normally look like, is it? I swear they are white tablets."

"It's because those are actually Oxycontin."

"Oxy?" Her jaw drops open. "Gray, what are you doing giving me prescription drugs? And why are they in this bottle?"

"You really didn't know, did you?" Tears fill my eyes and I blink them back. Wanting to stay strong even though I feel betrayed.

"Know what?" Anna asks, her voice barely a whisper.

"Patrick was having me distribute packages that had been tampered with to his VIP clients. I realized it the other day." I explain the water leak and having to repackage the bags that I dropped off at the center.

"That is why all of Patrick's clients are so upset," she says in a whisper. "God dammit, my brother was so stupid." She presses her hands to her face, choking back a sob. "His clients, they've been emailing and texting nonstop, asking when their regular shipment will arrive. All caps on REGULAR. I should have known something was sketchy." Her stream of consciousness lands on me. "How involved were you in this, Gray? How much did you know?"

I shake my head, swallowing. "I knew nothing. I swear. But now I feel like a fool." I press my fingers to my temples. "Patrick used me to peddle drugs, Anna. I trusted him and now someone is after me. They know I have them. Someone was in my garage."

"How much are we talking?" she asks.

"A baggie full. I should go to the cops. Maybe they—"

"No, don't do that. We are trying to get the police away from the company, not closer to it."

"I know, but I can't have someone in my house. What if they hurt my kids?"

"Are you sure someone was in your house?"

I tense. Why doesn't she want me to believe someone was there? I saw them. But it could have been Jeremiah. Couldn't it? No. I laid that theory to rest. If Jeremiah was close by, he would confront me. He isn't the type to hide in the shadows. His whole mode of operation is about being *in the light.*

"I think I should take you home, Anna."

"I don't want this to come between us," she says. "You're my friend, Gray. Hell, you're the one I called for a ride from the police station."

"Maybe you called me because you think I won't tell anyone about this. You think I am naive enough to believe everything you say."

"I'm not like my brother."

I don't answer, but I wonder how well she even knew her brother. Did she know he was sleeping with Treydon? She didn't know he was a drug dealer. And why does she want to protect the image of wELLEness, unless she still has a stake in the company — or wants one.

We drive to her house in silence, and when I pull up in her driveway she takes my hand. "I don't think you're naive. And I'm sorry that my brother used you. But I'm not him."

"Then why are you protecting the company?" I ask softly. "Why not just go with me to the police and give them the drugs?"

"Because I have sunk everything Jasper and I have in this company. He will kill me if he knows just how much. I can't have wELLEness go under, because then we'll be bankrupt."

"Like Karen?"

Anna nods slowly, realizing that I know more about all of this than she thought. "Yeah, like Karen."

"I have one more question," I say. "Why did you call me to come get you and not Marley or one of your new assistants?"

Anna gives me a half smile. "Because I don't trust them the same way I trust you."

I give her a hug, telling her we will get to the bottom of all of this, wanting to believe my own words. She gets out of the car, thanking me for everything.

Looking at the dash as I drive away, I can't believe it's only noon. For a day off, it sure feels draining.

CHAPTER 26

An hour later I have my slippers back on and am determined to enjoy the rest of my day off. Needing to feel extra cozy, I've got tomato soup warming on the stovetop, and am slicing cheese for a grilled sandwich.

When the doorbell rings I wish I had those fancy noise-cancelling headphones so I could act like I hadn't heard. I am not in the mood for any interruptions, even if it's well-intentioned neighbors dropping by.

I turn the soup down to a simmer and walk to the front door. Looking through the peephole, I'm surprise that it isn't Kendall or Luna; instead, it's Boone. Self-consciously, I look down at my fuzzy purple slippers and smooth down my hair.

Pulling open the door, I offer him a closed-mouth smile.

"Hey," he says, his voice gruff. His suit, though, is actually ironed, his collared shirt has a tie. And his hair looks like a comb ran through it at some point this week. "Mind if I come in?"

I lift my eyebrows, swinging the door open wider, curious. "To what do I owe this pleasure?"

He holds up a bag from Best Buy. "I brought a gift."

I laugh. "Uh, okay. And why did you do that?" I walk to the kitchen and Boone follows me as if we've done this before. Which, I suppose we have. But it feels overly familiar. Not in a bad way . . . just not in a way I'm used to. And definitely not in a way I'm expecting.

"You're making lunch?"

I bite back a smile. "I feel like you knew I would be."

"Not true. I didn't even know you'd be home." He takes off his wool coat and hangs it on the back of a chair. I swallow, my eyes landing on the jacket. "What? You want me to leave?"

"No," I say, flustered. "I just. I don't know."

"Okay, well, can I have a grilled cheese too?"

I laugh, sharply. In a good way. "Uh, sure Boone, you may."

"You know, my name is Orion."

"Like the constellation?"

He nods, running a hand over his jaw. Reminding me he made the same gesture last night, outside the brewery. A woman at his side. "My parents are hippies. My sister is Cassiopeia, but we call her Cassie." He shrugs. "You almost met her last night but you ran down the street like a chicken with its head cut off."

"Oh. That was your sister?"

Boone nods, watching as I spread butter on the bread, assembling the sandwiches. "She thought since it was the first Valentine's Day since my divorce I needed a night out."

"Was she right?" I ask, setting the sandwiches on a flat cast iron pan over the gas flame.

Boone shakes his head. "No. Cassie and I are opposites. I'm the introvert, she's the people person. I'd have been just as happy eating frozen pizza at my place."

"Why wasn't she out on a date?" I ask, curious about her. I can't imagine what I would have been like if I'd never ended up at Garden Temple, if my parents wouldn't have died. Would I have been single on Valentine's Day too? I'll never know.

"Her boyfriend is in London getting his PhD. It's a long-distance relationship that has disaster written all over it."

I laugh. "So she is also the optimist of the family?"

"Do I sound jaded?'

"More like bitter." I smile, then reach past him and grab a spatula from a ceramic vase on the counter, flipping the sandwiches.

"Who were *you* out with last night?" he asks, averting his gaze. He grabs the ladle from the vase and swirls the tomato soup. Standing side by side with him should feel strange. He is this authoritative man with power — similar to Jeremiah in ways that scare me, but different than him in all the ways that matter. But it doesn't feel strange. It feels good.

And that scares me more than anything else.

Stepping away from him, I grab plates, bowls and spoons. "Is it Detective Boone asking or Orion?" When he doesn't answer right away, I add, "It wasn't a date, if that's what you're trying to ask."

I turn, at the same time he does. We're face to face and this feels so different than being hip to hip.

His hands land on either side of my arms. Holding me still. I don't want to move. I want to stay right here, in this moment, a moment where my secrets are safe and his eyes are on mine. A moment where I'm not standing up all on my own. A split second where I let myself imagine being in this mess of my life with someone else.

"I am," he says, clearing his throat. "Trying to ask, I mean."

I step back, remembering my daughters and my past and Jeremiah. The bag of drugs in my room. All the things that would ruin this before it ever began.

Besides, I was a fourteen-year-old bride, pregnant by the time I was fifteen. A mother of three and not even thirty. A killer and a criminal, blood on my hands and too many lies to hide if someone were ever to get close enough to learn any of my truth.

"I'm sorry Boone, I can't. Can't go there."

He nods, dark eyes wounded, but he remembers himself quickly enough. "I'm sorry, I shouldn't have—"

I rest a hand on his arm. "No, don't apologize. Let's eat, okay?"

"Yeah?" Relief floods his face.

"Yeah." I smile, and carry the food to the table, pushing away the desire that I can't let grow into anything more than friendship.

We begin to eat and I ask what's in the bag. "You said you brought me a gift?"

He shrugs, wiping his hand on a napkin before pulling a box out of the plastic bag. "A home security system. Thought of you being here, alone. Just worried about you is all."

Emotions rise within me, his thoughtfulness toying with my heart in ways I've never known. Patrick was kind and generous, but I never felt any sort of longing when I was with him. Probably because there was no chemistry, no magic. Which makes sense now that I understand his relationship with Treydon. And makes even more sense now that I know my friendship with Patrick was about being used as his drug mule.

But with Boone it's different. He cares about me in a different way than anyone ever has before. And while I'm not in a place to let my life become intimately entwined with anyone else's — I do appreciate it. Because for my entire adult life I've been walking on eggshells, tiptoeing around a man who scared me when he looked at me too long, who hurt me when he touched me, who took away my innocence when I was still a child. I've never been looked at like this by a man, like I am something worth protecting.

"I could install the cameras, if you'd like?"

"That would be wonderful," I say, turning the box around in my hand before setting it on the table and picking up my spoon, wanting to take the subject away from me. "So, I brought Anna home from the police station earlier today."

Boone nods slowly. "How was she?"

"Pretty wound up. It's been a terrible few weeks for her. I'm just glad to know she isn't connected to the murder. I don't want to imagine a family doing that to one another."

Boone eats silently, clearly not eager to discuss the case. But I am desperate for more understanding. Part of me wants to tell him about the intruder this morning, but I'm scared. If I'm brought in . . . the glasswork walls of my life might start to shatter.

"Boone, if it isn't Anna, who is it? Do you have any leads?"

"I really can't say, Gray."

"Have you thought about Treydon? Because I wonder about him and Patrick—"

"Listen, Gray. I can't share details of the case with you, but believe me when I say we're not going to pin this on just anyone. We're looking at everything, and I'm going to do what's right. There will be justice, I won't stop until I make sure of it."

Orion Boone is everything Jeremiah wasn't. He has a strong moral compass and I just pray it leads him to the killer. Because until they are found, I won't be able to sleep without one eye open.

CHAPTER 27

After we eat, Boone stays to install the cameras on the house. "Might as well do this while I'm here," he offers.

He gets a ladder from the garage and I tense, wondering if there might be something incriminating there — but thankfully I dealt with the mess the other day.

"Damn, you have a lot of inventory. How long have you been selling this stuff?"

"A month or so. But Patrick brought a bunch over. I have more storage than he did at his condo."

"You know that condo of his is worth $1.8 million? He could have afforded a storage unit, don't you think?"

"Wow, that is a shocking number."

"What, more impressive than my cabin in the woods?" Boone grins, taking the ladder in one hand, and swinging up the garage door with the other. He's taken off his suit jacket and rolled up his shirt sleeves, his muscular forearms able to do the heavy lifting. I open the packaging of the cameras and hand him the electric drill.

He mounts a camera above my garage door, one on my front porch, and one above the back door. He does the hard work, I just give him the screws one at a time.

When he finishes, he pulls out the instructions, telling me what app to download. My phone keeps freezing though, and the App Store won't let me download it. "It was a hand-me-down from Anna," I tell him. "It's been glitching lately."

"Well, two options. We wait until you get your phone fixed, or I get the app for now so at least if anything shady goes down here, we will have evidence."

A chill runs over me. "You think something shady is going on at my house?"

He gives me a hard look. And I remember the first day he was here. The open back door. The empty Coke bottle on the kitchen counter. He knows I don't feel safe. Question is, does Boone know more than he is letting on?

"I think having extra security is never a bad idea. I'd hate for something to happen to you, Gray."

"Thank you, for worrying about me and the girls," I tell him, choosing, then and there, to trust this man. Deciding that I would rather Boone know all my secrets — if it means the girls stay safe — than the alternative. "And um, yeah, you should install it. Better safe than sorry."

It only takes a few minutes for it to get set up, and he shows me the app. As I am looking at a live feed of my porch from his phone, there is an incoming call. York.

"I should take that," he says, taking the phone back and answering. "What's up?" He tenses, and looks sharply at me. Then steps away, turning from me, and I run a finger over my lips. Whatever York is saying has Boone on edge.

He ends the call and takes a long exhale.

"Well, what is it?"

"It's bad, Gray."

"The girls? Olive, Ruthie? What happened?"

Boone cuts off my fears. "When is the last time you saw Anna?"

"This morning. I picked her up, I told you. And drove her home."

"When was that, Gray? Try and remember."

"It was noon. I remember looking at my clock on my dash as I drove away from her house. I was starving and drained. It's why I came home and made comfort food for lunch."

"What else?" Boone asks.

"Nothing. Gosh, why are you asking me about her? What's wrong?"

"There's been an incident."

I bring my hands to my face, covering my mouth and nose, desperate to remain calm. "What kind of incident?"

"It's Anna," Boone says. "She's dead."

* * *

It isn't something I ever imagined having to do. But after I text Sophie, asking her to babysit the girls after school, I get in Boone's car. Anna's husband Jasper had called ten minutes after Boone told me what happened and asked me to identify his wife's body.

"I'm getting on the first flight I can, but I'm in Singapore. I won't be home until tomorrow. I just need to know it's really her. That she's really gone."

Of course I told him I would, but now as Boone drives me downtown, it feels unreal. It was only a few hours ago that I was hugging her, and she was making sure I knew how much she trusted me. Now, she's dead.

Of course my first thought is to assume her and Patrick's deaths are connected. But it isn't until I arrive at the morgue and am shown her body that it hits me — brother and sister both murdered within a few weeks. This is no coincidence.

The coroner takes me back to a room where Anna is on a table. She's just arrived but there is a sheet draped over her body, and when it's pulled back, the room goes dark for just a moment. She is the third dead body I've ever seen and I pray it is the last.

Anna. Patrick. Him.

Tears roll down my cheeks as I take her in. Her face is just as I remember, flawless skin, soft hair, freckles on the bridge of her nose. But below her neck is a torso I don't want to see. She was shot twice, and I bite back the bile in my throat, wanting to be strong. Her brother is gone, her husband is halfway around the world — she has no one else. I need to show up for her now because there is no one else who can.

"It's her," I tell the coroner, the astringent cleaner burning my eyes. I leave the room as quickly as I came. It's too heartbreaking to see someone who took me under their wing gone. Dead.

"You okay?" Boone asks as I enter the lobby. I wipe the tears from my face and keep walking, out the doors. I don't want to talk. Not now. It all feels too raw. He catches up to me as I reach the passenger side of his car. He unlocks it and we both slide into our seats. "You're not going to like this, but I need to bring you in."

"In where?"

"To the station, Gray. You need to come in for questioning. Just so everyone knows what Anna's last few hours were like."

"I don't know what they were like. I was with you eating lunch."

"I know that, but it looks like you were the last person who saw her alive."

"Besides her killer, you mean?"

Boone nods. "Yeah, besides her killer."

"Fine. Of course, whatever you need. I'm just exhausted by all of this. And now, to lose her too, it's just . . ." I shake my head, hating how vulnerable I've been today in front of Boone. I need to rein myself in, not let myself fall apart. I run my fingers under my eyes, refusing to give into my emotions any more.

"I know. It's a lot. But you got this, Gray."

I turn my head ever so slowly, wondering why I am trusting this man I hardly know. Is it simply because he wears a suit and badge? Is that enough of a reason to let your guard down?

At the station I'm led into a room and Boone and York both follow me. York clears his throat. "I hear you were with the victim today?"

"You mean Anna? Yes, I picked her up here hours ago."

"And where did you and Anna go when you left?"

I frown. "To the coffee stand on 6th and Park. We got lattes and drove to the Ruston Lookout and talked."

"What did you discuss?" York asks. Boone clears his throat, leaning back in his chair, watching me intently. Does he not trust me?

"She said she was being asked a lot of questions in a roundabout way. She felt like someone was trying to get her to say something. Something she didn't understand."

"What about you, Gray?" York asks. "Do you know?"

"Know what?"

"Know what we are interested in?"

I swallow. Now is my opportunity to tell the truth. But I'm scared. And it doesn't help that Boone is staring me down.

York asks me again to explain the events leading up to me dropping Anna off at her house. What we discussed. What was said. He asks me in a dozen different ways and I run my hands over my face, feeling exhausted. I just want to go home. Be with the girls. Grieve Anna's death. To think for a moment in peace.

Boone lifts a hand and signals to the mirror on the wall, and I realize, with stupidity, that I am actually here being questioned. As a suspect.

"I need a lawyer," I say. "I need you to read me my Miranda rights, if this is about more than me seeing Anna before she died," I say. "I won't be taken advantage of, do you understand?"

"Gray, it's okay, we're done here," Boone says, looking over at York, trying to cool me down. But I'm not going to sit and talk when I know I have rights.

"You're right," I say, standing. "We *are* done."

CHAPTER 28

I leave the station and realize it's nearly dinnertime. Sophie was with the girls last night too, and guilt is creeping in. I need to get home. I pull out my crappy phone to get an Uber, but before I can, Boone is at my side. Telling me to get in his car.

"You're not getting in a vehicle with a stranger," he says.

I follow him, because I don't want to pay for a cab, and also, he's right. After Anna's death today I don't exactly want to be alone.

My stomach falls. Sophie and the girls are at the house by themselves. What was I thinking?

I bury my face in my hands as Boone drives and he keeps trying to get me to talk. "Just say something," he tries. "What are the tears about, exactly?"

"Exactly?" I finally shout. "How about the fact you think I had something to do with Anna's death? Let's start there."

"I don't think you had anything to do with—"

"Just enough to bring me in for questioning?"

"It's not like that, no one suspects you of anything," he says, exasperated. "If we did you would have been given your rights, God, Gray. Listen to me, I'm not the bad guy. I'm trying to help you."

"Why?" I ask as he turns the car down my road. "Why are you helping me?"

"Maybe because I care about you? Is that so insane?"

"Kind of," I toss back. "Because you don't know me. You know nothing about me and—"

"Fine," he says, screeching to a halt in front of my house. "Be like that. Pretend there isn't something here when we both know there is. Cassie told me I was being ridiculous to even consider — after everything — but I — God."

"Could you be more cryptic, Boone? I don't know what you are even saying anymore."

"It doesn't matter," he says. "Let's go make sure the girls are safe and then I'll leave you in peace. That's what you want, right?"

I nod tightly. My chin wobbling. "Yes, that's what I want," I tell him, not meaning it even a little. Not even at all.

We get inside and Sophie is with the girls at the kitchen table playing Settlers of Catan. Ruthie jumps up when she sees me and wraps her arms around my waist. Boone tenses at that, then gives a two-finger wave to Sophie. "All okay here?" he asks.

She nods, walking over to us. "I'm just in a losing battle over sheep and hay."

Boone's eyes meet mine and he nods back to the door we just entered. I tell the girls one sec and follow him. "I'm gonna head out," he says, running his hand over his jaw. "I know that got a little . . . intense in the car and at the station, but I'm worried about you, okay? I'm just gonna put that out there and you can do whatever you like with it."

"Thank you for the ride," I say. "And for the cameras."

He looks up at the cameras he installed hours ago. "If you see anything unusual around your house, let me know. I can check the footage for you."

He leaves and I close the door, resting my forehead against the wood frame for a moment before turning back toward the kitchen. I want to put everything on pause for a moment, but I can't. Not now. Not when everything feels like it hangs in a precarious balance, my entire life ready to topple if there is one more shake to this foundation.

* * *

The girls take turns showering, and when they are in cozy pajamas, I turn the radio to a classical music station and sit on the edge of Ruthie's bed, braiding her damp hair as Olive tells me about what they are doing at science club this week. I don't tell them about Anna because I want this day to end on a good note, and I feel an urgency to protect their innocence from more heartbreaking news.

"So we are gonna use microscopes and look at different products to see if there is a difference between the organic ones and the regular ones. I brought in some vitamins last week — don't worry, I didn't take anything new from the garage, only the stuff from the house. Ms. Peters is gonna send them to a lab."

My heart stops. Did she get her hands on Oxy? Did I keep prescription drugs only to let my teenage daughter discover them?

"What color were they?" I ask.

She scrunches up her nose, getting in the passenger seat as Ruthie climbs into the back. "The pill was yellowish? And the tea was more green. I don't know, it's just extra stuff we had in the bathroom."

"That's interesting," I say, relieved beyond measure that she didn't take the bottles from Patrick. Then, smiling, I add, "Oops, sorry. Not interesting. Don't want Tomas to get annoyed with me for using that word. Is eye-opening better?"

Olive smirks, then trades places with her sister so I can braid her hair also. "He isn't like that. He would never tell you what you can or can't say. Besides, I think it's his mom who is picky about the words he uses. He isn't weird or anything."

"I didn't think he was."

"His mom works at the school. She's the dean. So she hears whatever he says, and he has to be like, you know, on good behavior all the time? Like we used to be with Dad."

"Is that how you felt?" I ask. "Like all eyes were on you since you were the prophet's daughter?"

Olive turns, her hair pulling in my hand. "Of course. We could never mess up. Other kids would always tattle."

"But part of you still wishes you were back at Garden Temple? Even though you can see how it wasn't fair?" I ask, softening my words and straightening her head. I continue braiding as Ruthie looks through the stack of books I recently brought home from the library.

"I like going to school. And going to stores and getting hot cocoa at a coffee shop. And I like you being our only mom. But I miss things too. Like playing the piano at church. And I miss Abel."

"And your dad, do you miss him?"

Olive turns, looking up at me. "No, Mom. I don't miss him. And I think you were right in taking us away. You were really brave."

"Oh Olive," I say, pulling her into a hug. She has no idea how much I needed to hear those words form her today. She has spent so many months struggling with my decision to take her away from the life she knew, but she finally is coming to peace with it. "I love you."

"I love you too, Mom."

I tell the girls goodnight, kissing Ruthie's cheeks and whispering my I love yous. After turning off their lights, I get into the shower myself, washing away the day. The water is as hot as it can go and I exhale as tears fall down my cheeks, the grief of Anna's death causing me to fall to my knees, fear winding up my spine so tightly I don't know if it will ever unravel.

When I get out of the shower, my face blotchy, eyes red, I see several notifications on my phone. Wrapped in a towel I walk to the kitchen to get a glass of cold water, drinking it as I read the texts from Elle.

> Elle: *Sorry to bother so late. Heard about Anna. Heartbreaking on all counts. I'd love to see you at tomorrow's meeting at the center. It's important to stay close at times like this.*

Me: *I didn't realize there was a meeting.*

Elle: *It was for regional execs. But I know people would love to hear from you, as you were so close to both the team members we've lost. Meeting @10*

Me: *I'll try.*

Elle: *Sending you love and light.*

I walk up the stairs to my room, hating to call in sick at work, but also wanting to see what is going on with the company. Maybe I should just bring in the baggie of pills and confront everyone. See who else was involved in this on a regional level. And Anna wasn't a part of the drug circuit, she was about to take the Oxycontin, so why would someone want her dead?

After dressing for bed, I get under my covers, my head spinning with worry. Eventually I fall asleep, because when Olive calls for me, I jump with a start.

"What is it?" I ask, running to meet her in the hallway.

"I heard something. Someone. Outside in the backyard."

"You sure?"

"I'm sure."

"Stay here," I say, walking down the stairs and grabbing a knife from the butcher block on the kitchen counter. I can't end up like Anna. Like Patrick. I won't.

With the knife in hand, I flip on the back porch light, looking for someone. Anyone. Anything. But there is no one here. I fling open the door, shouting. "I know you are here," I scream. "I know you are watching!"

Then I look down, see glass on the steps, black pieces of plastic at my feet. Looking up, I see the camera smashed, broken entirely.

If they are coming for me, I have to figure out who it is. Boone might solve this case eventually, but I could be dead by then. We all could be.

CHAPTER 29

After a fitful night, I wake knowing who I need to speak with. While a large part of me believes the person who smashed the camera is connected to the drugs, I can't help but wonder about Jeremiah.

Is this paranoia or is it my intuition guiding me? How did his empty glass Coke bottles wind up in my kitchen twice? That is no coincidence.

Once the girls are off to school, I call in to work, letting them know I won't make it this week. I hate losing the hours, but I'd hate to lose this entire life I've built even more. They are understanding, and I'm glad I've been such a consistent employee because I've earned my boss's trust.

"I heard about Anna. I'm so sorry, Gray. You've had a hell of a month."

"Thank you for understanding. I'll be back next week. I just need to let this all sink in."

"You don't need to explain it to me. We will see you soon, take care."

With that taken care of, I pace my living room, getting the nerve to call Naomi again. Last time we spoke, she wasn't happy with me, called me a sinner, a disgrace. None of it surprising. I left the fold, the family. I didn't expect her love.

But she is also my only contact at the house this time of day. Lydia will be at the schoolhouse and Naomi will be home with the babies.

I dial the number to the house, and it rings three long times before she picks up. "Hello?" Her voice is soft like always.

"It's me, Naomi."

"Grace? I told you not to call. I don't want Jeremiah angry with me."

"So you didn't tell him I called last time?"

"No. I didn't want to upset him. He has enough on his plate." A baby cries in the background and I hear her shush him.

"How is Sadie?" I ask about her baby, knowing that's Naomi's favorite topic, and wondering if she has the same dark hair as her mama. As her father.

"She loves to cry," Naomi sighs. "Teething now, which, you know how it goes."

"I do. And you, how are you?"

"You really calling to ask about me?"

"I want to know how you are, but you're right, I'm calling about Jeremiah." I swallow, not sure how to phrase this, how to keep her on the phone. "Look, I know you don't want to speak with me, but I need to know if he was home last night."

"Last night? Bout what time?"

"Eleven?"

She clucks her tongue. "He was here all right. With Lydia. Heard them too, if you know what I mean."

My face reddens. We never discuss our intimacy with Jeremiah. "Oh?"

"Lydia had a bee in her bonnet, all upset because Jeremiah was over at Bethany Dale's house for dinner, took her for a walk after."

"Took Bethany on a walk or Lydia?" I ask, confused.

"Bethany. That's why Lydia was so upset. Jealous, I suppose."

"Jealous of what?"

"They're getting married, Bethany and Jeremiah."

My heart falls. Bethany Dale was Abel's best friend growing up. They would run to the creek and catch tadpoles. They'd play in the dirt piles behind the house, making roads for their toy trucks. They would take their bikes and ride around the compound for hours, playing chase. But now Bethany has been caught. By a man three times her age.

It's not right. And tears slide down my face, thinking of Abel, how he must feel at this news.

My son never told me who he wanted as a bride one day, knowing it would be ordained by his father, not his choice. But everyone knew Abel loved Bethany.

"Are you there?" Naomi asks.

"I'm here. Just thinking of Abel."

"I know," she says, her words gentle. "But you know it's God's will, not ours. And maybe Abel's desire for Bethany wasn't pure."

I want to scoff. Pure. As if Jeremiah's desire for a sixteen-year-old virgin is.

"So Jeremiah came home, after supper and a walk, and went to Lydia's room?"

"Yes, and he was there until this morning," she says, her voice more sad than bitter. "He walked out of her bedroom and came to the table where he ate the oatmeal I made. Why are you asking?"

"I thought maybe he had found me."

Naomi clears her throat. "I'm not trying to hurt you when I say this, but I don't think he is looking. I think he's moved on. Marrying Bethany is his way of putting you in the past, and pointing Garden Temple toward the future."

"What do you mean, future?"

"We're nearing the End of Days," she says more fervently. "Jeremiah says it's almost time for us to enter the Kingdom of Heaven."

"What are you talking about, Naomi?"

"You know what the End of Days means, Grace. It means we will be delivered soon, all of us. And that is why

I wish you were here, with the girls. We need to be together when the time comes, so we can spend eternity as one."

When I was with Jeremiah he always prophesied about God coming for those who were saved. He'd preach that our duty at Garden Temple was to rebuild the Garden of Eden for our Savior's return . . . but I never truly believed it.

I couldn't, not with my memories of a life in the real world. I saw it all as fabrications of Jeremiah's messiah complex . . . but Naomi doesn't see it the same way.

She's a believer, like so many others who live on the compound with her.

"I love you, Naomi. Keep your babies safe, okay?"

"May God keep you," she says before the line goes dead.

Tears streak my cheeks as I consider Bethany lying with Jeremiah, and it breaks my heart.

And when I think of Abel, learning of his father's decision, my heart breaks all over again.

Before I can wipe my tears away, there is a knock at the door.

I set my phone on the counter, thinking of the meeting at the center, how I need to get there and confront Treydon and Elle, ask what they know.

But first, I have to confess to Boone. Because he is here, standing at my front door.

CHAPTER 30

He's angry, I can see that. I open the door and he grunts, stepping inside. "The back door camera is down, Gray. You didn't call, didn't say anything. I drove over here as fast as I could. How could you—"

"I'm sorry. I was going to call. It was a long night is all."

He groans with frustration. "Someone took a bat to the camera. Who would do this? What aren't you telling me?"

"I don't know." I press my fingertips to my temples, scared. Because I do have an idea. And once I say it, things might change forever.

If it wasn't Jeremiah here, then that means it was whoever came after Patrick. Doesn't it?

"You know something. Tell me, you can trust me."

"Can I?" I ask, looking into Boone's eyes; they are pleading with me. He needs to solve this case, I can see it is wearing on him, and Anna's death just compounds his need to bring safety to the city he has promised to defend.

"You can," he says more gently now. "Look, I just saw the camera feed. There was some glitch with the app and I didn't get a notification until just now. I saw a guy in black coming into your yard, the next thing I knew the video was cut off. And I freaked out. I'm worried for you. I know there were other things happening here," he says.

"Things like what?" I ask, making him spell it out.

"The back door was open that first day. The Coke bottle that had you on edge. Your lies about your name. About your past. You know there's no information on you on record, up until a year ago? You didn't even file taxes."

I haven't filed taxes because this coming April will be the first year I ever needed too. But that is a hurdle I haven't had to cross yet, so I have avoided it. Until now. Until Boone.

"You want to start telling me the truth? Because I sure as hell know you aren't Gray West."

I hate that I keep crying, but I hate lying even more. This isn't who I am, who I ever was. The weight of keeping so many secrets weighs me down and I'm scared of falling. "Come here," I say. "I need to show you something."

I turn and walk up the flight of stairs, knowing that inviting Boone into my life might be a death sentence, but it also might be my way out. My way forward.

"What is it, *Grace*?" he asks. "I don't like games."

I turn, quick on my heels. The hallway dim, our voices reverberating as the walls cave in. "Don't. Call. Me. Grace. I'm Gray now. Gray."

Boone nods, lifting his hands in front of him as if to calm me. Warn me off. Back me down. He's probably worried I'm completely unhinged. And maybe I am. But so what? Maybe it's time I lose control.

"Why Gray?" he asks, the question sincere and not at all the one I expected.

I swallow, stepping closer. "Because I was taught that the world was black and white. But it never made sense. Because everywhere I looked, all I saw was gray."

"I get that," he says. "I do."

"Why? Why do you get that?" I ask, not believing he could understand where I come from, not at all.

"I had a little girl," he says, the words surprising me. "Ruthie's age. Suzannah was all sunshine and sparkles, really everything I'm not." He looks past me, seeing only memories. "Hell, maybe everything I was. She died three years go and a part of me died too. My wife, Taylor, she left because I'd become pieces that no longer fit." Boone shakes his head, running a hand over his jaw. "What do you do when the life that once made all the sense in the world suddenly feels like a never-ending rainstorm, a goddamn cloud that just won't pass?"

"You look for cover, anywhere you can find it." Tears prick my eyes and I see this man in front of me, broken in ways I understand, stuck in a storm that he never asked for but has to weather nonetheless.

"What I can't figure out, Gray, is what your cover is. Your story. Because you're connected to Patrick and Anna in ways I don't like, but you're not a killer. So what are you?"

He's wrong, of course. I am a killer. But I didn't murder either of my friends.

I walk to my bedroom and he follows. In my underwear drawer I reach for the bag of Oxycontin. Holding it up in my hand, the morning sunlight filtering through my window, the red pills are clear as day.

"Shit," Boone says, eyes fixed on the bag in my hands. I set it down on the dresser. "Why do you have this, Gray?"

I press my palms together, but I don't pray. I make a wish. Letting it take flight. Desperate for everything to turn out okay.

"I found it in Patrick's product supply. He was delivering it to clients." I pick up the bag, shake it, stepping closer. "I was delivering to his clients. Do know what that means?" I ask, shoulders high, hope lost. "I looked it up last night. It means I'm in possession with intent to distribute. I *have* distributed. And all I have to prove that I didn't know is my own word. And what value is there in the words of a woman whose entire identity is a lie?"

Boone looks at me with such grave concern, such intensity a shiver runs over me. "So arrest me, Boone. Take me in and tell my daughters that I'm Patrick's drug mule. A common criminal. A woman who's never even had a prescription in her life is peddling pills." I drop the bag on the floor, stretching my arms out toward him, daring him to cuff me.

He takes me by the wrists instead. Pressing my arms up, covering my chest. We're inches apart and tears roll down my cheeks, and pain wraps around my core.

He's holding me, I realize, so I don't fall.

"We know about the drugs, Gray," he says. "Patrick had a whole safe filled with them. We knew."

"You knew?" I ask, trembling. "I thought if I told . . . I thought my girls . . ."

"It's okay, Gray. The girls are okay."

"Someone is after me," I tell him.

"I know. And we'll find them."

"Did Patrick's drug dealer kill him?" I ask. Boone lets go of me, realizing I am past the point of collapse.

"I don't know yet. But we have guys trying to find out."

I take a long breath, running my fingers under my eyes. "Okay," I say; just knowing there are officers who know what is happening and are trying to solve these crimes makes everything less scary.

"Look, I have to take these. What are you doing now?"

"I'm going to the wELLEness center. A meeting Elle wants me at. They're talking about Anna and Patrick. I think everyone is pretty stunned, which makes sense. It's all so shocking."

"Will Treydon be there?" Boone asks.

"Maybe? I don't know. Why?"

"I think York is going to call him in for questioning again. His affair with Patrick makes him a suspect."

I nod, more relief flooding me, shame too, though. "I should have said something," I say. "He knows about the drugs."

"His alibi for the night of Patrick's murder checks out," he says.

"And Anna's?"

"That's what we're working on." Boone and I leave my room, going downstairs. The drugs are in his hand, he says he's going to enter them into evidence, and that he'll get a more detailed statement from me later.

He waits as I get on my winter coat and grab my purse and phone. "Call me if you need me. If you need anything at all."

I lock my door and we walk to my car. Boone waits for it to defrost. Once it's warmed up, I roll down my window. "Thank you. For not being like every other man. Thank you for being you."

I pull out of the driveway, not knowing what Boone is to me, what I am to him — but knowing that my heart is lighter after that conversation.

Now if only we knew who killed my two closest friends.

CHAPTER 31

When I step out of the elevator I'm stunned to see two dozen people in the lobby, mingling with mimosas.

I look around, trying to find someone I recognize, when Elle catches my eyes. She walks over to me, arms open, with two champagne flutes in hand.

"Oh darling, take this, you must be just exhausted."

"No thank you," I say, setting the drink on a high bar table. There are caterers manning a brunch buffet and servers carrying around trays of fruit kebabs. "I didn't realize this was a party. What's going on?"

"This is how the execs at wELLEness gather. It's important for all of us to have a positive mindset, helps us with alignment. In fact, in the board room there is a Chakra specialist offering vibrations. And a reiki healer in an empty office."

This flagrant lack of concern over the murders of two employees shocks me. "Elle, this isn't appropriate. Anna hasn't been dead twenty-four hours."

"I know," Elle says, resting an arm on my shoulder. "But she loved everyone here. She would want us to celebrate her."

"Her or your product line?" I ask, pointing to the banner with photographs of the latest wELLEness products hanging behind the buffet.

"Anna, of course. It's why I wanted you here as well. I'd love for you to say a few words about her, for morale."

"I don't know that I can."

Jasper, Anna's husband, joins us. "I just got in from Singapore," he says. "I came straight here. Elle said you were coming. I needed to hear from someone who saw her the day she . . . she . . ." His shoulders begin to shake as tears fill his eyes.

"Oh Jasper," I say as he begins to cry.

Elle's botoxed face fills with tears too, and suddenly I am giving them both hugs. Soon everyone is holding tissues, grieving the loss of a friend. When I first walked into the lobby I thought it was a business meeting, but I soon see it is a way for people who cared about Anna to congregate in a safe place.

Elle looks to me, and I try to put on a brave face, realizing that everyone here is as shellshocked as I am. Jasper's found a chair and is crying without reservation. I am surprised he came here straight from the airport, but maybe he is as lost as I am right now.

Marley, Anna's assistant, hands me a microphone and I clear my throat, looking at the company. "I'm Gray West and I was a friend of Anna's. She was a welcoming person who loved having a full house and friends around, which makes this tragedy all the more horrific." I press my lips together, remembering our relationship. "The first time I met her was at the library where I work. She was looking for a kombucha recipe and I directed her to my favorite resource. It was only six months ago, but in that time, she helped me get into a wonderful home, helped me survive the holidays as a recently single mother, and introduced me to wELLEness. It seems impossible that she's gone, that Patrick is too. Their friendship meant so much to me and I know it meant so much to you too."

I look over at Elle, who wipes the tears from her eyes, then takes the microphone from me. "Thank you, Anna. I'd love to invite anyone who would like to come forward to offer a few words of warmth on this chilling day."

I sit beside Jasper, listening as several women step forward, sharing memories of Anna and Patrick. Eventually the tears have all been shed and Jasper gives me a hug goodbye. "Her cousin is coming out to the house," he tells me. "I need to go. But we'll keep in touch, okay?"

"Of course," I say. After he leaves, I look across the room, wondering if it's time for me to make my exit too.

Before I do, Elle takes the microphone again and says there are a few business items to address before we all go, and Marley begins to hand out packets for everyone in attendance. I take mine, tucking it into my purse.

"Please read this at your convenience, it is also on the website, simply updates to some policies. But I don't want to make this about business. Today is about honoring the ones who have gone before us."

I leave in the next elevator and three other women slip in with me. I've never seen them before, but I can't help overhearing them.

"It's so sad, about Anna, but this new payout system won't work. I'll never make a profit with these margins."

Another woman flips through the packet in her hand. "Right? And I have so much inventory in my she shed my husband is already pissy about it."

"And do you see this, the only way you can make it to the next level is by coming to a wELLEness course? It's pay-to-play." Her eyes meet mine. "Oh crap, sorry," she says, shoving the packet in her bag. "This is totally not the time to talk shop."

The elevator doors open and we all step out. "It's fine. It's really not my concern," I say. Because it isn't.

As I walk to my car, I drop the packet in a trash can. I don't need to read it to know what it says. This is a pyramid scheme just like Boone warned. Pretty packaging wrapping up a scam where the Karens of the world end up losing.

And it isn't just the drugs that are the problem — I spent nearly two decades of my life in a cult, and I'm not about to enter the free world only to get tied up in another one.

Feeling freer than ever, I unlock my car. But when I slip inside, I gasp.

Because I am not alone.

CHAPTER 32

Treydon is in the backseat, directly behind me, shaking, a gun in his hand. "They're coming after me, Gray," he says.

"Who?" I ask, the gun's silver casing glinting. I force myself to look away. To look up at Treydon.

"The police," he says. "You need to drive. Drive, Gray!"

I reverse the car, leaving the lot as Treydon holds the gun to my head.

"Did you say something?" he asks.

I have to stay calm. I have to stay alive.

"They already knew," I tell him as patiently as possible. "There were drugs in Patrick's safe."

"There were? Shit." He groans wildly.

"Where do you want me to go?" I ask.

"Anywhere. I don't care I just . . . I'm scared."

"I get that. But you really don't need to hold a gun to my head to make yourself feel safe. I am not going to hurt you, Treydon."

I focus on the road, turning toward the only place that makes sense. I turn left, then right, hoping that Treydon's complete lack of control will keep him from seeing where I am taking us.

"I didn't kill anyone," Treydon says. "I didn't. You believe me, right?"

"I believe you," I say, not knowing how else to diffuse the situation. I consider the way I would talk to Jeremiah when he was angry. I'd placate him, tell him exactly what he needed to hear. "Of course you didn't kill Patrick. You loved him. And you loved Anna. They were good people. And so are you, Treydon."

"You think?" he sobs. "Even though I went along with Patrick's plan of involving you? You know what he said after you met him? He said, 'She's perfect. She's too stupid to know how dumb we think she is.'"

His words hit hard, because I cared about Patrick. I did. I trusted him. He was my friend. I stood up for him. Let him into my life, to know my girls. It's a gut punch to know I was so betrayed, and so easily.

I left Garden Temple to be strong on my own, and somehow let myself get caught in another man's lies.

"Patrick was cruel," Treydon continues. "And yet I loved him. And now everything is ruined. And for what? Who even owns the company?"

"What do you mean?" I ask. "Elle does. She says she never sold it."

"Anna said otherwise," Treydon says. "People think I'm not an asset, that I'm just an assistant, but I know things."

"And what do you know, Treydon?" I ask, pulling into the police station parking lot.

"I know that I'm not a killer." He realizes where I've brought him. His shoulders shake as he breaks down. "Do you believe me, that I never hurt Patrick?"

I nod. "Boone said your alibi checked out, Treydon. No one thinks you did this."

"Truly? I thought . . . I thought the drugs would make it look like I had . . ." He's crying hard, cradling the gun in his hand. He has become unhinged after losing Patrick, and if he loved him, I can understand the fear that has brought him to my car today. Fear driving him to do something reckless.

I did the same thing when my back was up against a wall. I didn't hold a gun, but I held something else just as deadly.

I kill the ignition and open the door, calling for help, shouting until an officer takes notice. "He has a gun, but he isn't dangerous," I cry out.

I tell them that Treydon is in the car, had me at gunpoint. And the cops rush in, yelling at him to drop the gun, to open the door.

Tears fall down my face, the intensity bringing me back to the afternoon when I became desperate, unhinged, willing to do anything to change my fate.

Treydon complies with the officers' demands, exiting the car with his hands raised high in the air. I stand watching, alone, until a moment later when Boone is rushing out the doors of the station. Wild-eyed.

"What happened?" he asks as I lean against my car, trying to catch my breath, running my hands through my hair.

I tell him about the meeting at the center, about Treydon being in my car. How he was frightened and felt so alone. Emotions I can absolutely understand.

"You're going to need to come in and give a statement," he says. "I'm sorry, but you have to."

"It's okay. I know." When I enter the station it is with less fear than last time. When I tell Truce my name as he fills out the report, I know Boone recognizes that it's an alias, but he doesn't say anything. And for that, I owe him nothing but gratitude. I can't open that case when this one still needs closing.

It takes longer than expected, but I suppose I've never been asked to give a statement on a man connected to a prescription drug ring who held me at gunpoint. Truce gets me a cup of coffee. It's terrible, but he's friendly. York, who seems too young for this job, calls me ma'am, which makes me feel too old considering I'm not even thirty.

These men terrified me only weeks ago when I met them at Patrick's condo. They were in uniforms then, with badges that gave them power, but they aren't holding it over me now. They are kind and concerned. They ask questions about the Oxycontin in my house and I explain it all in detail. How I found it after clients called complaining about the product they'd received. How I googled the letters on the pills to identify them. How I was terrified of being connected to this crime, which is why I hid them in my drawer.

How I know it was wrong, how sometimes doing the right thing is the scariest thing of all.

"What matters is that you're doing the right thing now, Ms. West," York says and at this, I smile. Ms. West.

For so long I've been looking for my true north. A compass. A direction that would lead me to where I'm supposed to be.

But maybe I'm already there. Finally. Right where I belong.

"I have to ask something," I say to the officers when they are done questioning me. "Who owns wELLEness? Is it Anna or Elle?"

Boone frowns. "Elle is the only person who has ever owned the company. Why?"

I look at the clock. Science club is getting out. "Just wondered," I say, standing. "But I've got to go. It's time for me to get my daughters home."

CHAPTER 33

The girls are surprised to see me at their school, picking them up from their club. But after the day I've had, all I want is to see their faces, to know they are safe.

They are in a classroom with about a dozen other students of various ages cleaning up from their projects. Setting microscopes in drawers and scales in cupboards.

Ruthie sees me in the doorway and runs to greet me. "Hi, Mom!" She wraps her arms round my waist in the unabashed way of a third grader, while Olive's eyes lift, meeting mine. She has the smile of a thirteen-year-old who is both embarrassed and pleased to see her mother at her school. There is a boy next to her, Tomas I am assuming, because he is looking her as if she's a treasure. "Let me get that for you," he says, taking the microscope from her hands. Her cheeks turn pink and she mumbles a thank you.

Their teacher dismisses them and the girls both meet me in the hall. "What's going on?" Olive asks. "Why are you here?"

"Just wanted to see you," I tell her, not wanting her to know about Anna's murder yet. Wanting to keep things normal for as long as possible.

"Well, you'll never believe what I discovered in science club," Olive says.

"What is that?" I ask as we walk outside to the car.

"Remember how I brought in some of your wELLEness stuff? Well, I brought in Glow-Up. It says it has organic milk thistle to make you have a better mood. But guess what? There wasn't any milk thistle in it. And Sleep-Tight is a tea, right? It says it has five grams of melatonin and horsetail in it. But there was like, less than a gram of melatonin and not even a trace of horsetail."

"How could you figure this all out in one meeting?"

"Mom, I'm really smart. And it's a STEM school, remember? I looked into this stuff the last few weeks." She laughs. "And I told you, my teacher sent a bunch of the stuff we all brought in to a lab."

"A lab?"

Olive nods. "Yeah, Ms. Peters says you have to validate your hypotheses and we don't have equipment to run all that stuff in class."

"And it was all fake?" The knot in my stomach unfurls as I realize the enormity of the lie I've been living. Selling my neighbors Moon-Masks and Sweet-Cheeks, when all the while what they've really received are placebos. The only people truly getting what they wanted were Patrick's VIP clients.

"Guess so," Olive says, pulling out a stack of papers. She runs her fingers down the page, showing me Glow-Up's list of ingredients. Titanium dioxide, Yellow 5 for coloring, lead, mercury. No milk thistle. Nothing organic. "Awkward much, right?"

I let out a small, sharp laugh. Awkward doesn't begin to cover it.

When we get home, I call Luna, asking if the girls can come over for an hour. "I hate to ask, but I have an errand that can't wait."

"Of course, I just got Olive some new sheet music. And Sophie's here with Kendall's daughter, they are making play dough."

Grateful in ways I can't quite explain, I take the girls over, promising to pick up pizza on the way back.

Then I back my car up to the garage and begin loading it with all my wELLEness crap. Karen was right, this is a bunch of BS. Once the car is crammed with tonics and vitamin water and bath salts, I lock the garage and drive away. Even though the car is loaded down, I feel free.

Looking at the clock, I decide to forgo a stop at the center, and instead drive straight to Dash Point where Elle lives. I don't want to cart this garbage up to the third floor. I can leave it in her driveway. Petty, maybe, but I don't care. I need this gone so I can wash my hands of everything to do with her company once and for all.

When I get to her house, I am once again taken in by the beauty of her home. It's so picture-perfect, even with the large rain clouds looming overhead. I park my car right out front, and begin to unload the boxes and bins.

It doesn't take long before her front door opens. She walks out in furry slippers, a large glass of white wine in hand, her hair blown out and her skin damn near glowing, wearing a luxuriously thick bathrobe as if she's standing in a spa.

I know her flawless face has nothing to do with her skin care line, it has everything to do with her cosmetic surgeon on speed dial.

"What in the world are you doing, darling?" she asks from the doorway.

I walk toward her, wanting her to hear the truth from me. "I'm done. With wELLEness, with you, with this entire company. And I want my money back for all the product I bought."

Elle frowns. "Oh, Gray, it's been a terrible few weeks for you. I understand that. Come in, let me get you a glass of wine." She wraps an arm around me, but I tense as she leads me into her home.

"No," I tell her from the foyer, not wanting to go any deeper into her world or her life. "I don't drink. And I certainly won't drink with you."

"What is that supposed to mean?" she asks, narrowing her eyes at me.

"It means I know the products you sell are fakes. You get away with it because the FDA doesn't have to approve vitamins or supplements, but you are literally lying to people, Elle. I won't be a part of this."

"You already are," she says, setting her wine glass on a marble-topped table. "It's too late. You can't just walk away."

"Why not?" I say. "I have proof that you are peddling lies."

"Proof?" Her words turn icy, and I falter for a moment. I was at gunpoint earlier today. I can't let this end with me in another altercation. But her tone is sinister, deadly. "I will not be blackmailed again."

It becomes clear then. "Anna. And Patrick," I say. "They were blackmailing you, weren't they? It was never about drugs. It was about your bullshit product lines."

"I won't go down like this. Not after everything I've sacrificed for this company."

"You know nothing about sacrifice," I seethe.

Elle steps toward me, backing me into a wall and I panic, scared. Remembering being pinned like this before. How I didn't think there was any way out, any way to be free until I carved one out for myself.

Elle squeezes my neck, and I realize her hours spent sculpting her body have given her strength I can't match.

"Anna and Patrick tried to take it from me, saying they'd go public — but Patrick's little side-hustle made an easy way out for him. Anna, of course, was harder to deal with. She was always such a drama queen." Elle laughs as I struggle for breath. "Kind of like you, actually."

"You killed them both?" I ask, my words a whisper as blood drains from my face.

She smiles. "Yes, my darling. And maybe it's time I killed you too."

Before she can reach for a weapon, I grab one of my own. I've done this before.

There's a plaque on the side table with the word 'Peace' carved into the stone and I grab it, knocking over her wine glass as I do. Shards of glass and liquid splash against her tiled floor. My fingers gripping tight to the plaque, I know this is my one and only chance.

I can't die. Not after I fought so hard to come from Garden Temple alive.

She thinks I am weak, pliable, a pawn. But I am not. I am more than a game piece in her company, more than a sister wife to Jeremiah. I'm a woman ready to fight back.

My arm lifts, and I smash the ironic plaque against Elle's head.

She stumbles back, blood pouring from her head, and she falls, shock on her perfectly manufactured face. She's screaming, but not for long. With her on the ground, I grab for the belt on her bathrobe, yanking it hard, and then bind her hands behind her back, tying her to the banister that leads to the second floor. The knots are hard, tight ones I perfected when I was a Girl Scout. Before Garden Temple, when my life was still sane. Back when I was free.

I'm free now, free again. And I won't let anyone tie me down.

I pull out my phone, and call Boone. "I'm in Dash Point," I tell him breathlessly. "And I have the killer."

CHAPTER 34

By the time the police arrive, Elle has passed out. An ambulance arrives minutes later, placing her on a gurney, trying to stop the blood pouring from her head wound. Truce and York are already marking a crime scene, and I sit with Boone, on the marble steps of Elle's perfect home, telling him everything.

"Anna and Patrick were blackmailing her, saying they would out her as a liar if she didn't give them the company. Of course Elle wasn't going down without a fight. After she killed Patrick, she thought Anna would understand she was playing hardball, but she and Anna fought, apparently Anna wasn't going to give in. So Elle killed Anna too."

"And how did you untangle all of this?"

I smile, looking at this man who knows me in ways I never anticipated, this detective in a rumpled shirt, with a messy past, who knows that I have secrets, who is willing to keep them, for now.

"It was Olive, actually. My daughter. Her science club." From my purse, I take out the paperwork from the lab that the club used to validate their findings.

"I'll take this," Boone says. "For evidence."

I look across the foyer, at the plaque, bloody on the glossy floor.

"You did the right thing," Boone says, as if reading my mind. "And you acted fast."

"She could die," I say, looking at all the blood on the floor of the foyer. I'd tied Elle up, but it soon became apparent that wasn't necessary; she was unconscious, folded over by the time the police arrived.

"It was self-defense."

"That matters in a court of law?" I ask, visions of me and Bishop Timothy making my memories clearer than I'd like.

"Of course it does."

"But there are degrees to self-defense, right? Who's to say Elle was truly going to kill me?"

"Your neck is already bruising, Gray. No one is doubting she was holding you against your will."

"Is that enough? Being held against your will?"

"What are you trying to ask?" Boone chooses his words carefully, slowly, but there is worry in his eyes. "What are you wanting to say?"

I think of my betrothal. My aunt and uncle had given my hand to Bishop Timothy. A man who was forty years old. Graying at the temples. But it wasn't just that. It was the way he looked at me. The way he smacked his lips, anticipating something. Me.

I was to be his bride and I couldn't bear the thought. I was fourteen years old.

Alone in his study, he'd stepped close enough for me to breath him in. Winterfresh and Ivory soap, and I couldn't be his wife. I wouldn't be.

So, filled with fear, I did what I had to do to get away.

I grabbed a heavy paperweight from his desk and smashed it against his head. Shocked, he fell back. Just like Elle. Thinking I was small, weak and way too naive.

He lurched up, grabbing for my legs, and so I hit him again. And again. Until he wasn't moving. Until he was dead.

I'd stood, shaking, scared in a way that sends a chill up my spine even now. Boone sits with me, trying to understand, but how can I tell the man who sees me as a woman filled with possibility that I am also a killer?

Was it self-defense if Bishop Timothy never laid a hand on me? Was it self-defense if he hadn't yet taken me as his child bride? I've looked it up online in the year since I fled Garden Temple. Of course I have, a thousand times. Trying to find a line in a law that would give me permission to kill before he broke the law. Before he broke me.

I've never found a ruling, a verdict.

But maybe it doesn't matter.

Jeremiah found me that day, in the study, blood on my hands and the bishop dead and he saw my fear, but he also saw my innocence, my purity. My desire to be loved. The hole in my heart that had been burning since my parents died in the car crash.

He said he would protect me. Always. He washed away the blood on my hands and told the congregation that it was a terrible accident, that the bishop had fallen, hit his head. But that God had revealed to him, in that moment, that I was to be his bride. That he would take Timothy's place and marry me.

There were questions for Jeremiah, of course.

"But I thought the doctrine said you would never marry?"

"I thought you said that you were to remain abstinent?"

"I thought the prophecy foretold a single man, who would be the father to us all?"

He had answers. A new divine revelation, a promise from God, a declaration from the heavens. He was to marry a girl who had been orphaned. He was to marry me as a display of great devotion for the lost among us, and those without parents could find a father in him.

Those at Garden Temple chose to believe. Because it was easier than telling themselves the truth — that they were living a lie.

Boone takes my hand and helps me stand, realizing I am in shock and in no place to say any more. Or maybe he sees that my shadowy past will bring truths to light that he doesn't want to face. Doesn't want to see. Because he wants to see me as a certain woman too, a woman who has space in her heart for him.

But I don't. Not now, maybe not ever.

"Thank you," I tell him. "For everything."

We walk outside, to my car. And I know he wants to say more. Say too much. Things I am nowhere near ready for.

"Can I call you?"

I bite my bottom lip, not wanting to lie to him. Ever. "How about I call you? When I'm ready?"

He nods, not asking for pieces of me that I can't give.

I get in the car and drive away, both weightless and weighed down. As I drive through town, I roll down the windows of my car, the wind lifting my hair, the chill steadying my pounding heart. When I get inside the house, I set down my purse and keys, and pull out my phone to call in the pizza order for dinner.

Before I can, though, I see a shadowy figure in the yard.

My heart stops. Fear in my heart, up my spine. No. I thought I'd finally finished this, the police are supposed to handle the criminals — so why is there someone here, watching me now? I cannot let this go on anymore. I'll tell this man I don't have the drugs — the police took them into evidence — that I have nothing they want.

"Stop!" I shout. "Don't go!"

This time, instead of running, he steps closer. Forward.

His body is one I recognize. It isn't a drug dealer after all. It's someone I know.

Head lowered, hoodie raised, I flick on the back porch light as he lifts his eyes.

It isn't Jeremiah. It isn't a criminal prepared to make me pay.

It's my son.

"Abel?" I cover my mouth, stepping closer. To him. Him. My firstborn, my heartbreak and my regret. The boy I left behind, the boy who is here. Who has come back.

"Mom," he says, his voice breaking in a way I understand all too well.

"What is it?" I ask. "Was it you all those times at the house? Why didn't you say something?"

"I didn't know how," he says, pulling back his hoodie. "I was scared. I wasn't ready."

"And now?"

"Now, Mom . . . now I need your help."

THE END

THE JOFFE BOOKS STORY

We began in 2014 when Jasper agreed to publish his mum's much-rejected romance novel and it became a bestseller.

Since then we've grown into the largest independent publisher in the UK. We're extremely proud to publish some of the very best writers in the world, including Joy Ellis, Faith Martin, Caro Ramsay, Helen Forrester, Simon Brett and Robert Goddard. Everyone at Joffe Books loves reading and we never forget that it all begins with the magic of an author telling a story.

We are proud to publish talented first-time authors, as well as established writers whose books we love introducing to a new generation of readers.

We won Trade Publisher of the Year at the Independent Publishing Awards in 2023. We have been shortlisted for Independent Publisher of the Year at the British Book Awards for the last four years, and were shortlisted for the Diversity and Inclusivity Award at the 2022 Independent Publishing Awards. In 2023 we were shortlisted for Publisher of the Year at the RNA Industry Awards.

We built this company with your help, and we love to hear from you, so please email us about absolutely anything bookish at feedback@joffebooks.com

If you want to receive free books every Friday and hear about all our new releases, join our mailing list: www.joffebooks.com/contact

And when you tell your friends about us, just remember: it's pronounced Joffe as in coffee or toffee!

ALSO BY ANYA MORA

THE SISTER WIFE DOMESTIC SUSPENSE THRILLERS

Book 1: THE SISTER WIFE

STANDALONES

MY HUSBAND'S WIFE

NOT MY BABY

THE PERFECT FAMILY

THE MOTHER

THE LITTLE GIRL I ALWAYS WANTED

THE GLENNMARE GIRLS

Printed in Great Britain
by Amazon

44074811R00108